Chapter 1

Dearest sister,

You are no doubt surprised to receive a letter from me. Indeed I am surprised to find myself writing one. Kitty is a good enough correspondent, I own, but the news I have bears a more delicate hand than she can offer. Last night, Denny surprised me in the night and whisked me away – oh, you must think me so very awful! And I now find myself writing to you en-route to a boarding house where I will meet my future husband. Oh Lizzy, I hope you are not too angry with me! I trust you most of all would understand what I saw in him. I trust you to know that I was making the right decision and I hope there exists no bitterness in you for what I have done. Do not think, dear sister, that I intended to take him from you. It was only that I knew you had other options in London, Mama assured me of it. In fact, I do not even feel the slightest bit of guilt, so it must be so. Oh, Lizzy, your youngest sister is to be married! I do hope to see you married soon too, dear sister. For the happiness I feel at this moment should be felt by everyone. I blush at the thought that I will soon have my wedding night with my delectable officer. Oh, Lizzy! How lovely life is! I am so glad of having ventured to Bath, Lizzy, and hope you find your happiness in London. Please do not tell a soul, I wish to make the announcement once I can sign my name: Mrs. George Wickham.

For now, you will find me as yours,

Lydia Bennet

Elizabeth's hands shook as she read it. Postmarked over a fortnight ago: she felt helpless to do anything. Contrary to what her sister's letter had indicated, Elizabeth was no longer in London but at Pemberley, a large manor outside of Lambton that was home to a young acquaintance she met in town. Miss Georgiana Darcy, a lovely girl of sixteen, had asked her along for the summer while her brother was away, hoping to share the beauty of her country mansion with a companion. Elizabeth's Aunt Gardiner had readily let her go with Miss Darcy, eager that she report every detail of Pemberley back to her.

"Your home, Miss Darcy, is but three miles from my hometown of Lambton," Mrs. Gardiner had said on the eve of their departure.

"Lambton I know well, Mrs. Gardiner. It is a lovely place with even more lovely people. Elizabeth and I will surely visit it, for my brother and I often go into town to shop. Mr. Henson's bookshop is a particular favorite of ours. I believe my brother has emptied his store three times at least in his attempt to increase his own library."

"Mr. Henson has been around longer than Lambton, it sometimes seems. Pemberley's library, I have heard, is the most remarkable in the country so your brother's diligence has paid off."

"He would be happy to hear it, Mrs. Gardiner. Thank you."

Thus far, the girls had spent nearly a fortnight at Pemberley, enjoying everything the house and its surroundings had to offer, thus the delay on Lydia's letter reaching her. Elizabeth, for once in her life, was at a complete loss of what to do. Her sister had run away with a man she barely knew and her friend, Mrs. Forster, was unlikely to have breathed a word of truth to anyone, not even her husband.

Elizabeth was taken aback by the audacity of Lydia's suggestion that she would be angry with Elizabeth for taking Wickham. She had indeed been fond of Wickham's company, but she by no means considered a future with him. He had been a friendly foot soldier stationed near her home, and nothing more. Now –he was the object of her family's ruin. She began penning a note to Mrs. Forster immediately, desperate to learn if she had any idea where they had gone. She could barely decipher one word from another as her eyes streamed with tears. Why had her sister decided to tell her? And why must the letter have arrived so late? For all Elizabeth knew, the worst fate could have befallen her youngest sister by now.

"Elizabeth! What is the matter?" Georgiana cried, having entered the room too quietly for Elizabeth to detect above her sobs.

"Oh, Georgiana. It is something awful. I'm afraid…well, I am at a complete loss for what to do."

Georgiana begged Elizabeth to tell her everything so that she may be of some comfort. By the time Elizabeth had finished her tale, Georgiana's face was just as wet with streaming tears.

"You know this man?"

"I do. His infantry was stationed in our town but was moved to Bath before I left for London. I hardly know a thing about him, only his name, and that my family's best chance is for my youngest sister to soon become Mrs. George Wickham."

Georgiana paled and before Elizabeth could even form the words to ask what was the matter –she fell to the ground, fainted in shock.

Georgiana awoke in her bed, surrounded by a flurry of maidservants hovering about and Elizabeth and Mrs. Reynolds on either side of her bed.

"It does not due to be so upset, Miss Elizabeth, she will be fine," Georgiana heard Mrs. Reynolds whispering just as she was coming-to.

"Mrs. Reynolds," Georgiana muttered in earnest, recalling what had made her faint. "Elizabeth and I request passage to the shore, immediately. You will write to them and get the cottage by the water ready, will you not? It need only be a short visit."

Elizabeth dried her tears and attempted to guess Georgiana's motive but refrained from asking with one motion from the speaker.

"Yes, ma'am," said Mrs. Reynolds, studying Georgiana's face before leaving.

"I will be content to sit with Elizabeth while you see to it, Mrs. Reynolds. You need not worry about my health, it was just one incident and I feel much better. Thank you, as ever, for your care."

When they were alone, Elizabeth's tears spilled freely down her cheeks again. She had finished the letter to Mrs. Forster but knew not what else could be done before she notified her family.

"We must move quickly, Elizabeth," Georgina said. "You have written to whom she was staying with?"

"I have."

"Then let no more letters go until we have ventured to the sea. I know where we will find her and the less people that know, the better."

"But what if they are married?" Elizabeth did not understand. There was nothing apart from notifying her parents if Lydia had become Mrs. Wickham.

"What if they are not?" Georgiana asked. The question hung in the air like cigar smoke on a cool evening. If they were not married –that would mean Lydia was ruined.

"We will extract her before anyone is the wiser," Georgiana said confidently.

"But how do you know where they are? How is it that you know Wickham?"

"I will save that story, I think, for the carriage ride," said Georgiana firmly.

Chapter 2

They were off before Elizabeth could consider what had happened and what they were about to do and the story that took the whole of the carriage ride for Georgiana occupied what was left of her free thoughts.

"George, you know him as Mr. Wickham, grew up with my brother and I. Of course he is of a much closer age to William than to me, and he and William and my cousin grew up so close you would think they were brothers. By the time I was old enough to be amongst them, their ranking had more of an effect than any of them would like to admit. George was the son of my father's steward and, although a favorite of my father, could hope to rise no further than clergymen of which my father set aside a handsome living for him in the rectory on the Pemberley grounds. My cousin, Fitzwilliam, is a second son of an earl and was therefore sent into the militia and of course my brother was to inherit Pemberley. They went their separate ways, as we each grew older, though after my father passed, it fell to the responsibility of Will and Fitzwilliam to see to my care. Wickham, upon my father's death, did not it as necessary to become a clergyman right away and wrongfully sold the living to another man. He came back to us from time to time and kept a friendly enough relationship with my brother, though now William would say that he never trusted him. It was two summers ago that George found me staying alone with my companion at the very Oceanside home that we travel to now. He appeared everything a lady would hope for in a man and confessed that, in vain, he was in love with me."

"In vain?" asked Elizabeth.

"The very question I asked him. And his answer was that his only desire in the world was to be my husband but that my brother would surely not consent, hoping for a better match for me. 'But what match could be better than that made in true love?' he asked. I agreed. For that's what every girl believes at one time or another in her young life."

Georgiana grew quiet and sad, and Elizabeth knew the story did not have a happy ending.

"True love exists, Georgiana. It is just more mature and slightly more complicated than it appears in fairytales."

"I hope that you are right, for both our sakes, Elizabeth. In any case, it did not exist in this one. He persuaded me –I am ashamed to admit it, to run away with him and enlisted my companion in aiding us. We were to be married, I was promised, in three day's time and surprise my brother. Wickham was to stay with us until then. I see now, but I did not understand then, that I got very lucky. My cousin, Fitzwilliam, took temporary leave and visited me. He had always been more carefree, more joyous than my brother to me and was less like a father and more like a friend. I told Fitzwilliam our plan once he promised not to breathe a word to Will and, you can guess, his promise was quickly broken as George nearly was when Fitzwilliam got a hold of him. I was sent back home before my brother even arrived. They did little beyond threaten him as the law was not invoked on account of my reputation."

Elizabeth cried the tears that she knew Georgiana must have already shed as she continued the story, lamenting the young girl's broken heart and worried for her own sister.

"My heart was broken twice in that incident, Elizabeth. For when my brother and cousin arrived at Pemberley to see that I was all right, I refused their company for two weeks. They had separated me from my love, I thought, and hated them for it. My brother, whom you will meet, I am sure, is much better suited to putting his thoughts and feelings down on paper and so slipped a letter beneath my door on the fourteenth day that I refused company. It contained truths I did not credit in my heart for weeks beyond that. Within, it detailed his negotiations with Wickham and a signed witness account by my cousin. Wickham never intended to marry me but, rather, to take me to a sham ceremony and hide me away from my family until he received the amount of my dowry or he would marry me for real in order to receive it directly. He did not love me: not as a wife, not as friend, not as a sister."

"Oh, Georgiana!" Elizabeth held her as she had comforted Jane in more difficult times, as she now wished to comfort and protect her foolish sister, Lydia.

"I was such a fool, Elizabeth."

"Don't say such a thing. As I am sure your brother and cousin have told you, you were young. Wickham is a deceitful, despicable character to have duped a girl. You were not even a young lady yet, Georgiana. You must see that now. No blame is to go to you."

"I try to see it that way now, Elizabeth, and mostly I succeed. But it is sometimes hard. It was not for running away with him or trusting a family friend that I believe I was foolish – I refer to not believing my brother or cousin who have cared for me most gently since my infancy."

"That is exactly what being young is for –to make mistakes and learn from them. And just look at you! You're a bright young lady who is using her knowledge to help others and you would never make the same mistake again. In your helping my sister and me, it is an endeavor to make sure that no one makes the same mistake that you do."

"Thank you, Elizabeth. I wish I had known you at the time. I no doubt would have been much better off with you by my side as my comfort."

"I, too, wish I could have been there. But you are so intelligent that you did not need me to draw the same conclusion."

"What kind of girl is your sister?" Georgiana asked, changing the subject from what had been to what was now.

"You two could not be more different, I'm afraid. Lydia is, for lack of a better term, a very silly sort of girl. She did not have the same benefit as my older sister and I were awarded of traveling to London to visit my Aunt and Uncle for long periods of time. Lydia and my youngest sister, Kitty, are the products of my mother's sole guidance. My father somewhat lost interest in raising so many girls and the youngest were allowed to run wild, in a sense."

"And what of your middle sister?"

"She is the stark opposite as the girl you are about to meet. Very serious, all logic. As smart as she is, she often misses the point of the simplest of life's truths."

"I hope to meet them all, in any case. It would have been very interesting growing up in such a household."

"No doubt you will meet them, though you finding them interesting is something I'm not so sure of. Tell me about your brother and your cousin."

Georgiana launched excitedly into the topic of her brother and cousin and Elizabeth found herself increasingly curious to meet them. The combination of wisdom, kindness, education, and good looks of Georgiana's brother intrigued her while the humor, kindness, and loyalty of her cousin captivated her as well. If it were any other girl than Georgiana, she may have not been so inclined to believe such praise. It also helped that Elizabeth was certain that it was not Georgiana's sole purpose to see Elizabeth married to either of them –her lack of a dowry, besides Georgiana's sincerity, assured her of that.

"You will get along with each of them splendidly, Elizabeth," Georgiana insisted. "William will greatly admire your intelligence and energy and Fitzwilliam will find you to be the most humorous person in England."

"I hope you are right, Georgiana. Though I'd settle for second most humorous."

Chapter 3

When the interior of the coach turned frigid and, despite the windows being tightly shut, the salty sea air crept through to assault the girls' sense of smell, Georgiana explained her rough plan.

"He was living very near our sea cottage, Elizabeth. It might take me a moment, but I do feel confident that I shall be able to find the exact location again. And when we do, I shall confront him whilst you get your sister."

"Will it not be very dangerous? I should have liked to sneak her out instead."

"Perhaps you are right. Let us spy on his house and see if he is there or not and we shall try to get your sister out without even seeing him."

"My sister will not easily be persuaded, I'm afraid. I think lying to her, unfortunately, is the safest route. If I can only keep a level head when I see her."

It was nearly dark by the time their carriage rolled up to the lovely seaside home that Georgiana had deemed the Darcy's "cottage" though Elizabeth thought that this term was rather misleading. It was a great deal larger than a cottage, for certain, and even larger than her home. But cottage, she owned, was appropriate for the style of the place. For though it was much larger than such places ran normally, the twists and turns of the cobbled roof, the nearly total vine coverage, and the squared windows made it seem a large, magical place, not stately like Pemberley had been. This seaside retreat was warm, cozy, and romantic.

"I love it, Georgiana. I think this is the most beautiful home I have ever seen. Or that it ties evenly with Pemberley. Never have I seen such elegance and comfort combined."

"Thank you, Georgiana. My brother tells me that our parents spent many happy years here. I am determined that this place is not marred by my immature decisions."

"You are too good and it is too beautiful to be possible, Georgiana."

Once they were settled (the household was expertly prepared for the ladies with only few hours' notice) and a simple supper was enjoyed, the girls made their way to what Georgiana remembered as Wickham's hideout.

"We are quite safe, I assure you. He is the only thing to be feared in this little sea town and he has more to lose dealing with me than I do in dealing with him."

"What do you think he would do if he saw you?"

"Now that I think of it –probably run. My brother and cousin leveled more than sufficient threats at him if he should be in the same town as me, let alone under the same roof. If he should see us, it would give him quite a shock."

When they arrived at a duplex, shabbier than its neighboring holds, Georgiana pointed to a window. "That would be the main sitting room and, with the lights on, I assume at least one occupant is home. Shall we take a look?"

They did. More cautiously than they had anticipated after their hurried departure and determined attitudes. Elizabeth muffled a loud inhale by covering her mouth and turned, wide-eyed, to Georgiana. She had been right –there, in the sitting room, were George Wickham and Lydia Bennet.

They were arguing, that much was obvious, but Elizabeth could not discern but a few words of their discussion. If she had to guess, it sounded like Wickham may have found out that Lydia had penned a quick letter to Elizabeth because she heard her name brought up more than once. Georgiana waved Elizabeth away from the window and the two convened a few yards from the household so that they were able to speak freely.

"She is younger than I imagined," Georgiana said, growing less courageous by the second.

"As young as you were, Georgie," Elizabeth said, patting her hand reassuringly. "Though she is not as strong nor clever. All will be right. And whatever is right, will be owed to you."

"What is to be done?" Georgiana said in a faint whisper. All the color had drained from her face and Elizabeth saw what she guessed was the same, sad young child that had been betrayed by a family friend and then (as she had thought), her own brother and cousin.

"Have faith, Georgiana. We are doing all that we can. Look around —we got here first. We are her only hope. Now, as much as I would like to burst in at this very moment and give Wickham a good piece of my mind, I think it is best that we wait. Tomorrow, we shall return and wait until my sister is alone. We need to get her out before anything should be done with him."

"I will write an express to my brother and cousin, then. What do you think of that?"

"I think it is wise. We will save my sister and they can deal with Wickham."

Chapter 4

There has never been a greater adversary than a good night's sleep, Elizabeth thought as she joined Georgiana at breakfast.

"We shall not speak of Wickham's indiscretions to my sister until he is well apprehended by your brother and cousin, Georgiana," she said as the tea was served.

"Why ever not?"

"I have given it a great deal of thought about how you reacted to your being rescued. It took you a great deal of time to forgive your brother and believe that Wickham had deceived you and time is not something we have a hand. My sister is poor, she has no prospects, and Wickham has nothing to lose in destroying her reputation. She, on the other hand, will do everything to be with him. Her and I have never been close and any attempt to convince her of something will be in vain. We must deceive her just as she has been deceived by him."

"I am beginning to understand you. She will not likely give him up, as I was not willing to do. And we could do nothing, unlike what my brother and cousin."

"I will attempt to save face but I am afraid of what I might say if she is too ridiculous."

"I trust you, Elizabeth. You will do anything to see your sister safe again."

Elizabeth trusted that someone was looking out for them as Wickham was, at that very moment, taking his leave of Lydia and explaining that he would not be back until much later that evening. Where he was going –he did not say, and he did not indulge Lydia though she begged him quite piteously.

They waited until Wickham was safely out of sight and Lydia's melodramatic tears subsided and gave way to exploring a catalog that Elizabeth assumed contained wedding dress patterns and fashions of the day.

"A Miss Abigail and Miss Anne here to see you, Miss Bennet," said the house butler to Lydia, delivering the girls' fake names. It did not matter in the slightest to Lydia whether or not she knew her visitors; she bade him to let them in immediately, making some comment about her being surprised that they had been her first guests.

Lydia was in a state of excitable shock when she saw Elizabeth and completely ignored Georgiana but for the showing off of her engagement ring that Elizabeth had to assume was a fake.

"But how did you find me?" Lydia said when she had finally come to her senses. "And what was the purpose of the fake names?"

"We wanted to surprise you," Elizabeth said, teeth clenched at yet another showing off of the engagement ring. "Georgiana knows Mr. Wickham and thought it likely that you were here. We've come to invite you to tea and to..." she made a point of acknowledging the dress catalog, "take you to Georgiana's private seamstress."

Lydia's eyes glazed over with excitement and Elizabeth knew that no more needed to be said in order to get her sister out, she need not even explain why she wanted her sister to bring a few of her things along with them.

Georgiana's brother and cousin will be here this evening, Elizabeth kept repeating to herself as she faux-smiled through Lydia's tale of running from Mrs. Forster. Georgiana, she thought, was doing a much better job than she. She had the energy to ask questions and make the proper noises as responses. Even adding phrases like, "Oh, how lovely," here and there.

"Lydia," Elizabeth finally said, "why did you not tell Mrs. Forster? Would you not have wished to wed in Bath instead?"

Lydia threw Elizabeth a sour expression and rolled her eyes when Georgiana was looking to illustrate just how exasperating it was to have an older sister. "At first, it seemed appropriate. But Mrs. Forster turned out to be such a bore, as George pointed out. She may have insisted that I wait for mama, in any case. I'd rather make the announcement as already married instead of making a big fuss about things. I used to think a big to-do would be the thing I wanted, but George has changed my mind. I only wish to be married –and as soon as possible."

They took tea at the Darcy's cottage while Georgiana sent servants to a few dress shops to maintain the illusion that they were expected. They need only keep Lydia entertained until her brother arrived.

"You don't think Jane will be too upset, do you?" Lydia asked once the dressmaker had made it clear that no cut or fabric could be more complimentary. Elizabeth need only look at Georgiana to muster the patience necessary to answer her sister with any measure of cordiality.

"Jane is far too good natured, Lydia. But I believe that everyone will be a bit...curious as to why they were not invited to the ceremony." It was the closest thing she had said to the way she really felt, but when Georgiana's eyes grew wide, she knew she had to add something. "But they will understand, of course. It will be a lovely surprise. And mother, undoubtedly, will be so happy. I'm very grateful that you told me, Lydia. And I'm even more grateful that I am here with you right now." Georgiana's facial expression relaxed and Lydia was pleased enough with what she had said to ignore her completely and try on another dress that was again deemed to "have been made for her."

It was Georgiana's time to shine when, at the second shop, Lydia insisted on knowing every detail of her relationship with "her George" to gauge whether or not she needed to view the young Miss Darcy as a threat. Elizabeth noted with amusement that Lydia relaxed considerably when Georgiana explained that they were family friends but required more assurance. "Was he always so handsome?" she asked Georgiana as a test.

"My mother always said that my brother, cousin, and Mr. Wickham made a fine trio, Miss Lydia."

"Perhaps I can convince George to pay your brother a visit since they were so close. But I have not heard him speak of your family yet, so I don't yet know if that is something he would like to do."

Lydia's cuts were less masked the more time went on, but Georgiana handled it with as much grace as Lydia showed ruthlessness. If Elizabeth could feel anything but anger, she might feel embarrassment.

It wasn't until the third dress shop that Elizabeth was at an utter loss as to what to feel.

"Georgiana!" barked a deep male voice from across the shop. Georgiana jumped, startled as much as the Bennett girls, but showed recognition. *Could this be Mr. Darcy or the cousin?* Elizabeth wondered. She studied him while he escorted Georgiana outside to talk privately. He was tall with a wide build and boasted a full head of messy brown hair. He was either growing out his facial hair or had gone without shaving for a day or two, and this dark mess of a shadow on his cheeks and under his nose made his dark blue eyes pop, framed on top by his dark curls that spilled down his forehead. He was tired, to be sure, but this did not wear on his determination. *This was Mr. Darcy,* Elizabeth concluded. Handsome, stately, and kind –she could tell by the way he addressed his sister. It was when Georgiana gestured to

Elizabeth and Lydia inside that she noticed something else – he was *furious*.

She did not have time to see this in person as he disappeared soon after looking at her, giving her a thorough once-over before kissing his sister gently on both cheeks.

"My brother has a temper, Elizabeth," Georgiana whispered to Elizabeth whilst Lydia prattled on about some dress or other. "But I have set him straight and we will talk later. He does not approve of the method we have adopted to see this through. He wishes that I had not taken the matter into my own hands, but I have insisted that we discuss it later. We (you and I) have set matters into motion and since our part is done, he must do his. He is meeting my cousin now and they will apprehend Wickham as soon as he arrives this evening. We will not have to keep this up much longer."

Elizabeth was relieved, though worried at the impending disagreement she was sure to have with her host. She was a few years Georgiana's senior and was only now beginning to think of the dangerous outcomes their actions could have caused, but she could not dwell on this long. It was not in her nature to think of negative things that were not reality. She preferred to think only of the past as it gave her pleasure and, of the future, as optimistically as possible. Otherwise –how was anything going to get done with any sort of enthusiasm or hope of purpose?

"My brother, though I know him to be the most gentle creature, does not always choose his words or tone wisely, Elizabeth. I would hate for him to anger you."

"I cannot, Georgiana, allow myself to be upset by anything your brother says. I understand too much how he feels. He worries for his young sister. We have much in common. He and I will understand one another soon enough, even if we do not see eye to eye to begin with."

"Lydia," Elizabeth said to her sister later in the carriage ride home, finding it necessary to interrupt her unceasing musings about how handsome Wickham would look in his red coat on their wedding morning. "Do you mind scrawling a note to him to let him know that you will be with us for supper?" Elizabeth knew that Mr. Wickham would never receive the note, but there was no harm in keeping up the pretense for Lydia's temporary sake.

"Oh, I don't think it's necessary. He won't be back until later tonight and, seeing how I don't even know where he's off to, he may deserve to wait for me. The butler will tell him that I am gone and he should not worry too much about me. In any case, he goes out nearly every day and this is my first outing. It has been very hard here without friends and he is so busy getting everything in order."

Elizabeth said nothing of her sister's desire to make her alleged fiancé jealous and frightful of where his intended might be but her refusal made no difference to the situation.

She felt some semblance of pity for Lydia over supper, as the meal comprised the last moments that she would think herself as happy and about to be a bride.

A disturbance by way of a commotion in the hall told her this was all over and Georgiana excused herself quickly to "see that her brother finds his rooms in order." Georgiana was back in seconds with a summons from Mr. Darcy to see Elizabeth. Elizabeth could not remember what she said to her sister before slipping out of the dining room where she left a ghostly-white Georgiana and a still-happy sister.

"Miss Bennet, I presume?" the same deep voice from the dress shop said to her from out of the dark corner of the hall.

"Mr. Darcy," she said more confidently than she felt at that moment, curtseying.

"I demand that we speak in private later, I have much to say to you and, I assume, much to hear from you. But that can wait. The matter at hand demands that I wait for an explanation. I have Mr. Wickham behind this door." He gestured to the door he stood in front of and Elizabeth noticed that light poured from underneath it. "He is bound and gagged and being monitored closely by my cousin, Colonel Fitzwilliam who has had too much of a history with Mr. Wickham to allow him to move a muscle."

"I appreciate your help, Mr. Darcy. Are the bounds necessary?"

"For now, I do not know what means are necessary. But I know it is better to scale back than to discover restraints would have been advisable from the start."

"If you wish me to speak with him, I don't know what I'd say. I never thought I'd see him again. But if you give me a moment…" It wasn't that she didn't know what to say. It was that she didn't know what she *could not.* There were all manner of things she had to say to Mr. Wickham.

"That won't be necessary. You may have an opportunity to speak with him on the morrow but, for now, I need you to speak to your sister. I apologize ahead of time for the subject I am about to broach but as you and my sister have taken it upon yourselves to see this through, you could not have thought to avoid it. My cousin and I have…put pressure on Wickham and we would feel comfortable stating that your sister remains uncompromised though they were in the same household for quite some time."

"That is…" she tried to quell the blush that she felt creeping up her neck. She had never had such a conversation with anyone, let alone a man; and a *handsome man* at that, "good," she finished. She was sure it was good, but she was not sure that that was the thing to say at the present moment.

"Taking into consideration the pressure that my cousin and I have placed him under, I highly doubt that he is telling a lie. However, if he is, and your sister is ruined, it means a quite different outcome. I need you to ascertain from your sister that he is telling the truth."

"If he's not?" She did not look forward to speaking with her sister on the topic. Lydia was unruly, flighty, and, their father had always said *silly*, but there was more to it than that. Reckless. A great deal of time would pass between Lydia finding out that she would be separated from Wickham before she would answer any of Elizabeth's questions. It would most likely take a matter of days. And, though she did not know him well, Mr. Darcy did not look like a man to be trifled with. Nor did he look like the type that would settle for a matter taking days instead of moments to resolve.

"Miss Bennet, I would love to sit down. If you would be so kind as to follow me into my study." He looked suddenly ten years older, exhausted and at the end of his rope. He paused for a moment at the door before which he had stood guard. "Fitzwilliam," he whispered through the crack in the door he made, "I will be return shortly." Elizabeth did not mean to peer into the room, but her eyes were drawn to the only source of light in the hall like a moth to a flame and, inside, she saw the cousin, broad shouldered and intimidating, and Wickham —sweaty, tied down, and *bleeding*.

I shouldn't have looked, thought Elizabeth, *why did I look?* She suddenly didn't want to join Mr. Darcy in his study.

He noticed her pale complexion immediately, for it lit the way to his study brighter than a torch and, for a complete lack of comforting words, he gently placed his hands about her shoulders and guided her. She was shaking, he found, and he wished there was something he could say to comfort her. Though highly improper, she did not seem to mind the contact and he was too tired to care and, though contrary to what she may have assumed her reaction would be if this man touched her, she found it relaxing. Warmth radiated from his hands down her back and up her neck and, despite knowing that she should warn him against such conduct, she did not see that it mattered much, *not tonight.*

He guided her to a well-cushioned chair and poured her some foul smelling drink; the stench of which she was sure wouldn't leave her nostrils for a fortnight.

"Strong enough to deal, but not to forget," he said, raising his own glass in a bizarre toast. She attempted to go about this business with the same carefree attitude as he, and failed miserably when the drink made its way down her throat like she had swallowed fire. She coughed and spluttered but managed to keep it down, feeling the warm pass to her stomach and an odd, settling feeling with it. By the time she had cleared her eyes of the onslaught of tears, Mr. Darcy was before her with a tall glass of water.

"Thank you," she said hoarsely.

She blinked back more tears as the remainder streamed down her face and her eyes focused on his —big, blue, and gentle, for the moment. His eyes were the type she had only read about: expressive and alluring, but either captivating or cutting depending on mood.

"Was that your first?"

Assuming he meant the drink, she nodded between sips of cold water.

"You took it better than my first, believe me. My voice couldn't go above a whisper for two days; I coughed and spluttered so much. It doesn't taste good, but the warmth that spreads throughout is a clever friend, is it not?" She did not want to agree but she did. It was a lovely feeling, and one that was much appreciated after such a day. "I will not pester you about your relationship with Wickham, he has told me all that he knows of you and your family. I am sorry that the sight of him gave you quite a shock. My cousin and I are not cruel people and could not have harmed him —even after what he did to my sister. The injuries you saw were self-inflicted, of sorts, when he broke a window with his face in an attempt to escape when we confronted him. The window broke easily enough, but the same face he used to shatter it also broke his fall. He was never the most intelligent creature." Elizabeth did not wish to voice how much this revelation calmed her. "That being said, if we had used violence, we would have wasted our energy. My cousin and I have known since we were very young that Wickham could only be motivated by money, not pain."

Mr. Darcy propped himself on his desk and faced Elizabeth with a rather more softened expression than what had been directed at her before.

"Miss Bennet, it is late and you and I have had a long day that will only get longer. Let me put it plainly. There are two possible outcomes that will be drawn from the conversation you will have with your sister tonight. If her maidenhead is still intact, we must decide what actions to take that Wickham does nothing like this again and we must cover up the potential damage he has done your sister already. My cousin and I will do everything we can to send him to the United States or to Australia, depending upon what we can prove him guilty of. If, however, he has ruined her –then there are two options, neither of which I am fond. She will be made to marry him, or another husband must be bought for her. Your father, in the least, must get involved at this point and it will not be as tidy a matter to clean up."

Elizabeth remained quiet for a long while contemplating the possibilities. Neither, of course, was good. And she was sure that there would be much more problems to answer to once this first matter was clear. First of all, Mr. Darcy himself. She could still feel his anger, seething under an enormous weight of exhaustion, exhilaration, and responsibility. She would have to answer to allowing Georgiana to be in danger and would most likely never see the lady again.

"You have said that you believe Wickham is telling the truth? That my sister is…still a maid?"

"Yes. He has given me cause to believe him. I am surprised, but he seems to have not meant her to be so for much longer."

Elizabeth shuddered. "My sister will not easily be talked out of Wickham's hold, Mr. Darcy. She is young, ridiculous, and has never been one to listen to reason. I must get the answer from her through lies –she cannot know that he is being held here or that her answer will mean that she will marry him or not. If she is not ruined but finds out that her...maidenhead is the only thing standing in her way of it, I believe she will lie to me."

"Is she so foolish?"

"I'm afraid so. I must secure the truth through deception. I will continue the charade that Georgiana and I have created until I have my answer and then... I'm afraid she will have to be locked up."

"I have a room ready. Two rooms, that lock from the outside, ready for the both of them."

She wanted to thank him, but knew it was not the proper time. He was too angry with her to hear it. *Under any other circumstances,* she thought, *we could very well have respected one another.* She hoped that he relaxed enough to allow her Georgiana's friendship.

They exchanged strained pleasantries and went their separate ways; Elizabeth, to the dining room, Darcy, to again patrol Wickham's quarters.

Elizabeth was grateful when, upon a few minutes after her return, Georgiana excused herself under the guise of needing to speak with her brother. Of course Elizabeth could not have broached the subject with Georgiana in the room, but now that she was gone, she didn't find it any easier to begin. *Let the words come,* she told herself, *Lydia is not perceptive enough to see that it is not in your nature to say such things.* She and Lydia had never been close –it was always Jane and

Elizabeth, Lydia and Kitty, then Mary on her own. But Elizabeth could not appeal to Lydia as she was used to doing so with Jane. She must stoop to adopt more of her mother's tact.

"Our mother will be very excited, Lydia," she said, half-heartedly.

"I know. She always thought Wickham so handsome. She told me once, though in confidence, that she always wished to marry a soldier. And she will get such a kick out of her youngest being married!"

"Of that, I am sure. She did always think he was handsome, he will have the happiest mother-in-law in all of England, to be sure."

"And, as a married woman, I will introduce you and my other sisters to other men –officers and the like. And we will all be married to handsome, red-coated gentleman though I think Mary might protest at first. But she is so silly sometimes; I hardly know what she means when she decides to say something. Kitty will be so terribly jealous! I can't imagine she'll speak to me for a month."

It went on and on like this until Elizabeth could not bear adding comments like, "Oh, that is true," and "I never thought of that," here and there to make it seem as though she were paying attention. The moment had finally come. Elizabeth drew in a large breath of air and held it.

"Has he kissed you?" she asked innocently, letting the matter build.

Lydia had the decency to at least blush before answering in the affirmative and then added, "Well, really, I kissed him the first time but, since, he has instigated. I have hardly seen him these past few days, he has so much to prepare for, he tells me. But we will have plenty of time for time alone on our honeymoon, of course."

"Of course, the honeymoon. Well," Elizabeth pretended to stumble upon the matter at hand, "you have been waiting for your wedding night, haven't you?"

"Of course, Lizzy. It wouldn't be half as romantic to elope if you did not! It is not as though I've wanted to wait, truly. And surely Wickham did not. But I convinced him that it was better that way. In any case, I think it's helped him speed the process along and I'll only be married sooner which I would prefer."

"Of course, I'm sure you'll be married soon enough." She was more relieved than she could have imagined but it was only the beginning. This had been the easy part.

"Lizzy, it is getting quite late, I should venture home before Wickham really begins to worry."

Oh, you are the last of his worries, Elizabeth thought. "You stay here, I will find our hostess and arrange for a carriage and escort you home."

"Thank you, Lizzy. You know, you will make someone a very good wife one day."

Elizabeth bit her lip in an effort to mask how greatly she didn't appreciate the compliment from her baby sister and disappeared to find Georgiana or Darcy –whoever appeared before her first.

In a few moments wandering through the dimness of the hall, she found both of them in front of "Wickham's door."

"Miss Bennet?" Darcy asked her, too tired to ask his sister to excuse them for the moment.

"Wickham told the truth."

"You are sure?" He looked relieved but cautious.

"I am absolutely sure, Mr. Darcy. She is asking for a carriage to the boarding house, what is to be done?"

"My cousin and I will have to go and speak with her," Darcy said. "Wickham is bound and will be fine on his own, there's no way to break free."

"I would like to come with you," Georgiana's small voice perked up, strong though mousey.

"Georgiana, I hardly think that would be appropriate."

"William, it is most appropriate. In fact, it would be more so if I went alone to speak with young Miss Lydia for it is I who has the most to say about her present situation." Darcy looked to Elizabeth as though he wished to blame her for this sudden wave of independent thinking, but did not have the chance to say anything. "But the three of us will do fine and, in the very least, you will help to escort her to her room if she resists."

"Georgiana, this is a delicate situation," Darcy attempted to dissuade her again.

"Very similar to the one I found myself in not long ago. Though I have grown an age since."

It wasn't until Mr. Darcy's eyes met hers that Elizabeth realized that she was beaming and she did her best to hide her smile seeing as how the gentleman was not coping well with his younger sister's becoming mature.

"Elizabeth has been a godsend, brother. She has assured me of what before I was too afraid to believe and I would like to do the same for Lydia, if possible."

With little protest from the Darcy's cousin and a short introduction between he and Elizabeth, she was left alone to sit in her room, worry, and wait. She could hear no other sound other than her breathing, and this scared her the most. *Why isn't Lydia screaming at the top of her lungs as I expected of her?*

Nearly two hours passed before Elizabeth heard a tentative knock at her door and opened it to find Georgiana.

"I knew you'd be up. My brother said not to wake you, but I insisted that you would be up, waiting and worried and I only wished to put your mind at ease."

"That was very kind of you, Georgiana. You were absolutely right, I have been worried sick. Why could I not hear Lydia's protests? Is this cottage so large?"

"There were very little protests, you would have been proud of your sister. I don't know if she would have behaved the same way if you had been there, or if I had not been, or whatever other combination, all I know is that I was surprised and impressed. There were plenty of tears, reasoning, arguing, bargaining, to be certain, but she did not throw a tantrum as I half-expected. We all carried out our parts very well if I should say so myself."

This late night talk reminded Elizabeth of similar moments she had shared with Jane and this comforted her more than she could express.

"So what is to be done?" Elizabeth asked after Georgiana went into detail about their discussion, how Lydia consented to breaking off her faux engagement and resigned to do, more or less, what they asked of her because it would cause her the least amount of embarrassment. Elizabeth could not believe that Lydia understood all of the implications that accompanied what she had done but hoped she would in time.

"My brother wishes to speak with you in the morning but the most practical thing to do is to move to London or Pemberley, at least. We will meet in the morning first without your sister and then bring her in once we've hammered out the finer details. I cannot thank you enough, Elizabeth."

"What ever for? It is you –your family, who has saved me. Saved my family and, quite possibly, my sister's life. I cannot thank you enough."

"I am grateful beyond reason that I was in the position to be of service to you, Elizabeth. I wished to thank you for believing in me, for speaking to me so sincerely. You have instilled within me a sense of esteem that I had missed before. I have never been looked upon as an equal by my brother and cousin before tonight, nor has anyone ever looked up to me as Miss Lydia had at the table."

"I am so happy to hear it, but can only say that you have had it in you all along. If not for me, you would have discovered it in your own time."

They shared a tender hug and parted in order to catch a few hours' sleep before they were inundated with all the decisions that morning would bring.

Chapter 5

"Miss Bennet, no doubt I am in your debt for what you have done for Georgiana," Mr. Darcy said to her in his study after breakfast. "I have not seen her so happy in quite some time. It is especially impressive under the circumstances."

It had occurred to Elizabeth that she had never seen Georgiana so submissive or quiet as she was in her brother's presence, which at first she found odd owing to how much each obviously cared for the other. Now she realized that Georgiana was simply acting the younger sister, not wishing (in part because of her own shyness as well as for her brother's sake) to show that she had grown up —the younger sibling protecting the elder from his worst fear. Elizabeth, through no direct attempt of her own, had helped spring Georgiana from her shell and embrace the inevitability of her coming of age simply by being herself; a mature and grown young woman.

"I only wish I could make you see how much your sister's friendship means to me, Mr. Darcy," Elizabeth said. "This is one of the many reasons you cannot possibly owe me any thanks. You and your family have saved my sister's life. I cannot help but feel as though something greater than chance was at work here, bringing Georgiana and I together when I would most need her. It is such a wonderful coincidence, though the situation itself was unfortunate, that your family had known so much of the whereabouts and actions of Mr. Wickham. I do not want to think of what would have become of Lydia or my family had I not met Georgiana. Please do not say you owe me anything, Mr. Darcy."

Mr. Darcy did not intend to be impressed this morning when he set out to secure a private meeting with the Miss

Bennet this morning, but even he had to admit that he was. He had wished to thank her for making Georgiana happy and, before she joined them, make it clear that he wished her to leave with her younger sister as soon as possible. It was not only the business with a runaway sister that upset him, nor Wickham's involvement, it was simply that, now that he had seen Georgiana with a young woman, he realized that he could not trust anyone with his sister. Mr. Darcy was too versed with the women of the *ton* to wish that his sister turned out anything like them and he did not want any questionable influences around her at this so crucial a part of her becoming a lady.

When Georgiana had first described to him all the noble characteristics of her new friend in a letter, he had been overjoyed that she had finally made a connection with someone near her own age and so he had eagerly consented to her inviting the 'Miss Bennet' to stay with her at Pemberley whilst he remained in town. His heart grew when Mrs. Reynolds, his housekeeper, had written to him to personally extend her thoughts on the young lady and to assure him that Georgiana was in exceptional company. But now that he was faced with it –with *her* (though he saw nothing wanting in her character or manner), he mistrusted Miss Bennet. She was older than he had supposed, she spoke more assuredly than he had expected, and he knew nothing of her family or status. What could he have been thinking, he wondered to himself, to allow a stranger into his home and into his sister's life? The last companion he had assigned her was partially to blame for the trouble with Wickham and *her* references had checked out. What of this Miss Bennet who had no references?

Georgiana would understand, surely, when he asked both Bennet girls to return home. He would allow Georgiana to write to her and their correspondence would come to an end soon enough. He would find her more proper friends, ones that befitted her station for, although he knew nothing of Miss

Bennet's background, he could assume from her dress that it was not equal to theirs, especially as he had never heard their name either in court or in town. The matter of Miss Bennet's education still puzzled him for he found her far too bright to be a simple country girl as her sister, Miss Lydia, seemed to be. Once she was sent away, he would ask Georgiana what she knew of Miss Bennet's household and his curiosity would be satisfied.

Colonel Fitzwilliam and Georgiana interrupted them then in order to understand what was to be done with the rest of day.

"Miss Bennet," the Colonel addressed her, "we were introduced so hurriedly last night that I did not even extend a proper greeting. You must forgive me; it had been a long day. I know that we have much to do this morning, but I would like to say that I look forward to knowing you better as it looks like we'll have time to do."

Elizabeth smiled widely as he made himself comfortable, rather preferring his attitude to his dour cousin's. He was not as handsome as Mr. Darcy, to be sure, but his easy smile certainly made him more attractive.

"Now, Darce," he said, "quit looking at me as though I am at the root of all this and get on with it. What's the plan?"

Elizabeth was surprised that Darcy took this jest with such grace but supposed he must be used to it by now. She was *not* surprised when he did not respond with his own quip, and instead continued on as though his cousin had not said anything.

"Being that this a unique situation, I have come up with a skeleton plan but require your input as we all have different parts to play. I suggest we more or less take this day-by-day. I would like to depart later this morning for Pemberley after we send letters to those that we are aware know of Lydia's disappearance with a cover story. While this is being done, Colonel Fitzwilliam or myself will ascertain records from the boarding house official about the damage done to the window, this will be one of many evidences against Wickham of which we need proof. Fitzwilliam, I need you to go to see Colonel Forster in Bath to see that Elizabeth letter is received well and her story is corroborated. There, I hope, will also be evidence to him owing some place or other and you must find out where he was before that."

"He was in Meryton, Mr. Darcy," Elizabeth said, "very near my home where we met him. He was in London for a brief time prior and during, if that helps."

"It certainly does," Colonel Fitzwilliam encouraged her.

"Good," Mr. Darcy said firmly, startling Elizabeth somewhat. "Country expenses can be easily overlooked in the major courts but if he owes anyone in London, it would be taken more seriously. And, Miss Bennet, you must write to your family and construct some story or other about you having run into your sister and to let them know that you will be travelling home together." He shot Georgiana a look as though he would protest, but nothing more was said on the subject.

"I will explain the plan to Miss Lydia, help her with her side of the story and ascertain if there is anyone whom we owe a letter of explanation," said Georgiana, standing up and folding her skirts down. Darcy looked at her with a fixed expression, Elizabeth noted, as though he did not recognize her fully. Elizabeth looked to Colonel Fitzwilliam to gauge his expression and it was, she thought, for the same reason, surprise at Georgiana. He seemed bemused, she thought, pleased.

"She's grown in a day, hasn't she?" Colonel Fitzwilliam mused once she had gone. "Miss Elizabeth, I am convinced you are the most valuable companion."

Elizabeth enjoyed Darcy's soured expression before finding it necessary to respond. "I cannot say I am, for my own part, but I can assure you that Georgiana is my most cherished friend. I have not had a more happy summer than the one I have shared with her, this situation aside. She is a remarkable young woman."

"Are there more Bennets besides yourself and Miss Lydia?"

"I have four sisters, Lydia included. I am the second eldest, Lydia is the youngest and nearly of an age with Georgiana, though their similarities end there as you have noticed."

"Nothing that discipline will not tend to, I think," Darcy said with a stately air in his voice that Elizabeth did not like at all. *His idea of parenting is treating everyone forever as children.*

"Discipline may cure silliness, I am sure," answered Elizabeth. "But a heavy hand does not a grown up make. It is freedom out of guidance that makes a fully functioning member of society, Mr. Darcy. It is not that there is something wanting in her, it is that she was not ready to be faced with such a decision."

Darcy remained quiet though Elizabeth was sure by his expression that he wished to argue with her. Lydia and his sister had more in common than he wished to admit, she saw, and this realization was a sour pill to swallow. No matter how much discipline was forced upon someone, it could not guarantee that they would make the right decisions. After all – his sister had made nearly the same mistake.

"Five ladies?" Colonel Fitzwilliam attempted to continue as though the tension in the room was not there. "Darcy, I think a visit to the Bennet household is a necessity, especially if they are all so beautiful as this Miss Bennet."

"You are too kind, Colonel Fitzwilliam."

"A visit may be in order in time," Darcy interjected solemnly. "For now, we must attend to the matters at hand."

The next three hours were enough to make all of them wish to end their day immediately but there was still the matter of leaving the seaside. They piled into two carriages, Elizabeth, Lydia, and Georgiana in one while Mr. Darcy and Wickham sat silent in another. An exhausted Colonel Fitzwilliam left on horseback towards Bath but he did not envy the Darcy his journey. Elizabeth had stolen a moment with her sister before their carriages were loaded and found her a sullen, but not sulking, image of her former self.

"Lydia, I would understand if you aren't pleased with me, but I am confident that you will one day understand." She knew not else what to say. As angry as she was with her sister for sneaking away with a man she barely knew, it was her age and his cunning that were truly to blame. She –*they*, were lucky that Lydia had written to her. "It is important to remember that none of this was your fault." She didn't know how else to phrase it so long as her sister refused to speak, but she felt the need to say it. Wickham was much older, he was a practiced liar, and she was a fifteen year old who's only crime was to believe in love so much that she wished to surprise her family with her happy news. All in all, her only true crime was being young. There was no malice in her actions, only naivety.

"Elizabeth, in time I will speak to you. Georgiana has offered me a great amount of comfort but I am still unable to determine what I feel." It was spoken solemnly, as Elizabeth had never heard from her sister before. Georgiana had already explained that letters would be sent to those who knew of Lydia's disappearance and, to make a long story short, it would generally circulated that Lydia and Elizabeth had planned to meet up as Lydia was bored of Bath and learned that her sister was relatively close. Everyone but their father would easily accept the story, finding it easier to hear what they were told instead of consider the matter. Elizabeth wondered on the carriage ride if their father must be made aware of the situation and decided to speak to Darcy and his cousin about it if she could not come to a decision herself. She felt that she should tell Mr. Bennet, but only if she could guarantee that her father would not punish her. Lydia had suffered enough and a penalty might only drive her to other actions of ignorance before she had time to grow. If nothing else, her family would know a very different Lydia come home in comparison to the one that had left.

Chapter 6

"We're home," Georgiana said looking dreamily out the window. Elizabeth felt as relieved as if the nightmare was over when she saw the great walls of Pemberley. It was by no means her home, but the happy days she and Georgiana had spent there were too memorable to not feel just as comforted by the sight as she would Longbourn.

"It is beautiful!" Lydia squealed, nearly as lively as her old self. She and Georgiana had played games for the last length of the trip while Elizabeth half-slept, listening with glee to the sound of her sister's giggles. *Everything will return to normal,* she thought as she smiled at the sight of the property.

The ladies were taken in first so that Darcy and his staff were able to secure Wickham without an audience and Georgiana took Lydia to her room while Elizabeth rested in hers.

"My brother, I think, has calmed considerably," Georgiana told her in confidence once she had been admitted to Elizabeth's room after leaving Lydia to hers. "I have ordered your favorite dinner, I hope Lydia shares your love of it. I know my brother will be very excited."

"I wouldn't be so sure, Georgiana. Your brother will hold me accountable for putting you in danger. I cannot blame him, his protectiveness is overwhelming but it is hardly a fault. I was so distraught; I did not even think to wait for anyone to help. I was convinced that I alone was Lydia's only hope."

"Elizabeth, who knows what would have transpired had we not acted? I am no longer one to sit about and wait for news. You don't strike me as that type either. In fact, we proved that we are not. If we had waited for my brother (it pains me to say this), he may have refused to help you. Too much has happened for him to hold that against you and, if he tries, he must hold me accountable as well. I do not agree with him saying that he will send you and Lydia home once this is cleared up. I would like for you to stay and I would not mind if Lydia did also. I will speak to him on the subject."

"Georgiana, I do appreciate it."

"However?" She giggled, knowing Elizabeth was about to wax poetic about how she disagreed.

"I can do nothing against your brother. He has been too much help to me to deny him anything he wants and if that includes my sister and I going away, then I shall consent."

"But it is not for the right reasons, Elizabeth. My brother is not thinking of your interests or those of your sister, he thinks he is removing a poison from his sister's life of which he knows nothing about. He mistrusts you, God knows why."

"Perhaps because I allowed you to get entangled in this mess."

"He knows I had just as much to do with this as you."

"He will never admit to that. I am a great deal older."

"But I am not stupid, and neither are you. He was ecstatic when I wrote to him of our friendship but I am afraid now that it was out of selfishness."

"He only wishes to see you happy, Georgiana."

"As long as I am happy on *his* terms." *She's right,* Elizabeth thought and wondered immediately why she had been defending him a moment before. "Now that he sees me happy, he wishes to send you away and construct a replica; he will send me to town to make friends that he deems proper companions. He will make me a little cage, slightly bigger than the last, but one that I will soon outgrow. It does not occur to him that I will only become unhappy again if he dictates every aspect of my life. I was young enough, once, to make a huge mistake. I am old enough now to have learned from it, and make significantly smaller ones, if any at all, in the future."

"I think you should speak to him, Georgiana," Elizabeth said. "This goes beyond the matter at hand."

Chapter 7

Georgiana did not enlighten Elizabeth as to when she would speak with her brother, but she could easily pinpoint it when Mr. Darcy's looks of scorn turned into gazes of utter contempt. To her relief, the girls were left alone for the most part, even at mealtimes, though Elizabeth never received a report about what had been said.

Lydia improved in mood everyday though fell quiet and pensive at times. As Georgiana had said, Lydia looked up to her and Elizabeth saw that she did her best to shadow their hostess's every courtesy and manner. Elizabeth looked on with satisfaction at this, even more so when she thought of how Darcy would take it.

Three days after their arrival, Colonel Fitzwilliam appeared from Bath, bringing the news that all their efforts had proven successful and that, now, they must need only worry about getting records of London debts and Meryton debts (if they existed) which meant that the happy party would be moved to London the following day. Georgiana admitted to Elizabeth later that evening that her cousin had suggested to herself and brother that they leave the ladies behind at Pemberley whilst they attended to the matter but that Mr. Darcy had rejected the idea, saying that the matter was to be completely resolved. She had then been asked to leave and Mr. Darcy and Colonel Fitzwilliam were locked away in the master's study long before supper and long after the ladies had gone to bed.

It was not until breakfast the following day that the ladies were made to understand what was to be done and, though Elizabeth could not guess, she knew that it must be something in Georgiana's favor, for Mr. Darcy would not so much as meet her eyes all morning and barely spoke to his own sister.

"We will be departing on the morrow, ladies," Colonel Fitzwilliam addressed the Bennets and Georgiana between messy bites of his fifth scone.

"Oh? Not today?" asked Georgiana.

"No —and when I say we, I don't mean you. I just mean myself, your brother, and Wickham. We have decided to let you rest since there would be nothing much for you to do in London and having Miss Lydia out of sight while we see to it that Wickham is charged with crimes will be a caution we would like to take. You three will get along splendidly here and we are confident that the nightmare will end in London, after which you may join us."

Elizabeth looked between Colonel Fitzwilliam and Darcy during Georgiana and Lydia's expressions of gratitude and excitement. Mr. Darcy did not look up from his plate and, though the scones and eggs were the best Elizabeth had ever tasted, he looked down at them as if they were contemptible, inedible bugs.

But why, she puzzled, *was he so miserable?* He is an imposing man, far above the station of his cousin and more powerful than many. Why does he bend to the desire of his cousin and sister if he believes them wrong? She knew he did not lack the backbone to refuse them —she had seen as much in his eyes. Mr. Darcy was not to be displeased, disrespected, or disobeyed —but was he so stubborn as to have a temper tantrum when he was forced to admit that others' ideas were better than his own? Could he not admit when he was mistaken?

Elizabeth could imagine it now: selfish, obtrusive, stately Mr. Darcy was rarely challenged. His life was easy —he saw to everything in it. But now that a situation was out of his control, now that something included more than himself and his sister was growing too old to be controlled, he could only act as a child. This was hardly fair to others but it was mostly unfair to himself, for it was a miserable way to lead an existence. She no longer wondered as she had before why such an eligible catch was not married; the word "particular" did not even begin to describe him.

Chapter 8

Elizabeth lie awake, unable to sleep, too energized by the enormous relief that the nightmare was almost at an end. The following morning, if she saw Wickham at all, would be the last she saw of him. She donned her robe and moved silently through the house as she had so often done while she and Georgiana were the only occupants besides the servants, to find comfort amongst the shelves of the Darcys' great library. She had not attempted such a feat since they arrived back from the seaside, for Georgiana had intimated that a late night in the library was also one of her brother's habits and she could not have stood to run into him that way. The less she saw of Mr. Darcy, the less they could offend one another and the more likely she would be allowed to maintain a relationship with Georgiana.

Elizabeth lit a small fire in the great hearth centered amongst the countless volumes and moved amongst the rows slowly before picking up a Greek tragedy. It was her old custom to recline on the couch until the last of the embers burned and then choose either to put the book away or take it up to her room so as not to waste the firelight or unduly make more.

She knew within the first ten pages that she had chosen the wrong book for she had already woken up with her face pressed against the pages more than once while the embers still glowed bright. By page twenty, she resolved, she would go back upstairs.

A small noise startled her awake and she, dropping her book, found the fire nearly all gone out. The last *pop* of the fire, she thought, must have jolted her awake and she returned the book quickly to make her way back up to her room, her candle nearly completely out.

She was halfway to her room, she calculated, when the candle went out completely and she was made to feel her way along the darkened corridor until her eyes adjusted. She was nearing her door, she thought, when a large hand closed over her mouth and she was picked up and carried through the hall before she could begin screaming through her assailant's fingers. She heard some small commotion nearby but could not call to whoever it was and so began to struggle and kick, believing herself to be in the arms of Mr. Wickham.

Darcy, who by no means a sound sleeper whilst Wickham occupied any room of his house, was the first to rise and find himself at Wickham's door to find it *empty*. Darcy's heart fell into his stomach and he called aloud for Georgiana, screaming into his cousin's face just as Colonel Fitzwilliam rounded the corner.

"Gone?!" They both sprinted headlong to Georgiana's room, finding her just outside her doorway looking confused and scared.

"He's not with you?" Darcy said, pushing past his sister to peer into her room, finding it empty.

"Who? Wickham? Has he gone?" she gasped, turning white.

"There was a scream…"

"Elizabeth! Or Lydia!" Georgiana cried and followed her brother and cousin down the hall.

"Darcy, you check for Miss Bennet," Colonel Fitzwilliam dictated from the front, "Georgie, Lydia. I will go outside, he must be headed there."

It was quickly ascertained that Elizabeth was the one missing but this did no good –there was no sign of either missing persons that Darcy, Georgiana, or Lydia could see.

Elizabeth freed her right arm and leveled a hefty punch straight into Wickham's left eye, causing him to growl and half drop her. Only then did she remember his cut and bruised face, realizing that her hit may have done major damage. She kicked and punched wildly as he wrestled to pick her back up and overtook her after receiving three powerful kicks to the groin and a punch in the stomach. He limped in the darkness to the doorway, muttering all the while between hits suffered by Elizabeth. She clawed at his face and hair and screamed when his hands were not around her mouth but she still found herself in his clutches under the night sky, the outside brighter than in.

"Shut the bloody hell up!" Wickham shouted as she clamped her fingers around a clump of hair and ripped a good chunk of it out. His screams sent a flock of birds flying and he, for once, looked down at his prey to level with her directly.

"Georgiana, if you do not..." he stopped in shock. "Georgiana?"

Elizabeth punched upward towards his face and broke his nose, making blood pour and splash at every angle. She was drenched by the time he dropped her and, in her confusion, she could not understand why two men were now yelling and why Wickham was now a wrestling, moving mass on the lawn ahead of her. When her vision cleared, she saw Colonel Fitzwilliam dragging an unconscious Wickham back towards her and his hand outstretched to help her up. When she did not reach out to take it, he leaned down.

"Miss, nothing's broken, is it?"

Elizabeth found she could make no answer for, as the adrenaline dissipated and her vision returned, the pain came. She was afraid to speak and found breathing more like a stab in the chest. Beyond that, she did not think she could move her face, suddenly it felt fat and bruised.

"Hold on," he said gently. "Hold on."

A second and third figure, Darcy and Georgiana, followed by Lydia came bounding towards them.

"Elizabeth!" shouted Lydia and Georgiana in unison.

"Don't touch her!" urged Colonel Fitzwilliam.

"Was she aiding in his escape?" asked Darcy, out of breath.

"What?" Colonel Fitzwilliam shouted. "You are a fool, cousin. Look at her!"

"How else could…" Darcy began

Colonel Fitzwilliam interrupted him with a blow to the face. Darcy reeled, but instead of returning, glared at his cousin with the one piercing blue eye that he was not covering, now swollen and bruising. "Take Wickham inside," he growled and when Darcy made a sound that registered to Fitzwilliam as the beginning of protest, he screamed: "Now!"

Fitzwilliam knelt beside Elizabeth as Darcy disappeared inside with Wickham and whispered, "I don't want you to move, Miss Elizabeth. I will pick you up very carefully, and you must mutter at me when something hurts. Do not attempt to speak, just trust me." This would have touched Elizabeth had she not been in so much pain and, before she was fully in Colonel Fitzwilliam's arms, she passed out clean from the pain and events of the night.

Chapter 9

"An apology, to be certain! In the very *least*!" the sound of the not-so-distant quarrel reached Elizabeth. She heard shuffling to her right but could only listen, not yet look.

"Gentleman, please! Both of you will have to make an apology if you insist on carrying on like this just outside her door." The hushed whisper sounded like Lydia, but Elizabeth was sure it did not sound like something Lydia would say. The arguing ceased and Elizabeth fell back into an uneasy sleep, dreaming of a deep pain in her chest that she could have sworn was real.

"I will allow my brother the satisfaction of having the watch," Georgiana was whispering. "Since he has managed to anger every honest person under one roof he must do more to have it done away with. I cannot believe the way he has been acting."

No one made an answer and though Elizabeth thought it only a matter of minutes that had gone by since hearing Georgiana utter these words, she finally opened her eyes, one more than the other, only to take in the sight of a perfect stranger, *a doctor,* she reasoned, with Colonel Fitzwilliam, Darcy, and Lydia in his wake.

"Good morning, Miss Bennet. I am Doctor Mordock, and I don't know if you could hear me, but I was just explaining to these gentlemen here that your rib is healing very nicely. Do you find that you are having trouble breathing?"

Georgiana appeared with a cup of tea while Elizabeth negotiated shaking her head; it no longer hurt to breath as much as it had. She attempted to speak but when it only came out as a gurgle, the doctor continued:

"Do not worry about speech, my dear, give yourself a moment, but you are a long way already down the road of recovery. You have some lovely nurses here, I must say. Very attentive, I am told you have not been alone one moment. Not to mention the very concerned gentleman you see hovering about my shoulders, who have insisted I am here more often than I have attended to any other patient. You will be right as rain in no time, I promise you."

"I cannot thank you enough, doctor." She could hear Darcy saying as he and Colonel Fitzwilliam led him out the door.

"No thanks necessary," Doctor Mordock said, "just let the poor lady heal, the matter is out of my hands, I promise you. The bruise around her eye will fade in time; her rib will be good as new. She will be fine, and very soon. The gentleman she laid her hands on will recover nearly as quickly, I will have my statement to you by the end of the day."

"What are they talking about?" Elizabeth wheezed, not recognizing the gravelly voice that she emitted.

Neither Georgiana nor Lydia could make an answer, but instead sought to embrace or kiss Elizabeth where they knew she was not hurt.

"Oh, Lizzy!" Lydia began. "Wickham tried to escape and take you as a hostage."

"Doctor Mordock is the last testimony we will need to send Wickham out of the country," explained Georgiana.

"But I wasn't his hostage," Elizabeth pronounced slowly, "he thought I was you."

Georgiana paled considerably at this and excused herself to find her brother, leaving the Bennet sisters alone.

"How could such a handsome man be so terrible, Lizzy?" Lydia asked.

"We shall have to settle for ugly, good men, don't we?"

Georgiana returned with the gentlemen to find the Bennet ladies in hysterical laughter.

"It's nice to see you smiling again, Miss Bennet," Colonel Fitzwilliam said, making himself comfortable on the chair next to her bed. Darcy wandered about the room, unsure whether or not to sit down, and not sure where to sit if that's what he decided.

"You say that Wickham thought you were Georgiana?"

"Yes," Elizabeth struggled to get the words out. "It was the moment before you caught up to us that I learned it. He grabbed me in the dark and did not realize until we were outside that I was not her. He called me Georgiana when he told me to be quiet and paused when he looked down at me. That was I broke his nose and he dropped me."

"Doctor Mordock said he suffered from quite a hit, multiple hits. He thought I had done them and hardly believed me when I swore that I only delivered the punch that knocked him out," Fitzwilliam explained, laughing. "His medical advice, he said, beyond anything else, was to keep on your good side." Everyone joined in his laughter but for Mr. Darcy. "You'll see it's true because my cousin is not laughing," Fitzwilliam added, "for he is not on your good side and will own that it is not ideal."

Darcy shook his head disapprovingly and steadied his gaze at Elizabeth. "I am sorry for accusing you of breaking Wickham out, Miss Bennet. My worst fear had come to light that night, I jumped to another, far worse, conclusion. If Wickham thought he had Georgiana, then I have no qualms sending him to Australia. The United States, in my opinion, is out of the question."

"Where were you when he grabbed you, Elizabeth?" asked Georgiana, still getting over the shock of learning that it could have been she that was dragged away, kicking.

"I was reading and on my way back to my room from the library when my light went out and I was grabbed in the dark."

"We heard your scream," Mr. Darcy said.

"Then I wonder how you could have thought I was aiding him, Mr. Darcy." Elizabeth was beginning to understand that Darcy was too quick to think the worst of people but she did not want to think of him in the same light. *No wonder he is so miserable! He looks out at a blue sky only to search for rainclouds.*

He had the decency to flush scarlet and Elizabeth said no more on the subject. Perhaps, if nothing else, this may award him a lesson in humility. *To think of those other than himself,* would be too great a feat.

"The doctor has cleared Wickham for travel and so we will be on our way to London shortly, Miss Bennet."

"As much as I would have liked to avoid being attacked in the dark and dragged across your home, I am happy that my suffering will at least secure us safety from this day forward."

"You are braver than the men in my infantry, Miss Bennet," Colonel Fitzwilliam marveled while his cousin studied the grounds outside the bedroom window, afraid of saying anything.

Elizabeth was left alone —completely, once she assured her sister and Georgiana that it was best, but she soon found that, even with Dr. Mordock's concoctions, sleep would not come and, as soon as she resigned herself to that fact, there was the slightest knock at the door.

"Miss Bennet?" It could not be —but it *was*. Darcy's low voice whispered again, imploring her to allow him entrance. She smoothed over her blankets and cautiously bade him enter.

He crashed inside, dropping most of the books he was carrying. She moved to help him, but he gestured for her to stay.

"Please, Miss Bennet, I shall answer for my own clumsiness." He seemed less sure than usual, nervous – perhaps even humble. "Georgiana told me that you greatly enjoyed reading and since you will be unable to venture down to the library for the next few days, I brought some of it to you."

"That was very kind of you, Mr. Darcy, how can I thank you?" If this was as close to an apology as she would get from Mr. Darcy –she'd take it. She had a weakness for books.

"As thanks, you could not criticize my choices, I suppose," he said, a small smile grazing his face. *Was this a sense of humor?!*

"Oh?" Elizabeth wanted to see what else she could draw out of him. "Must I be so lenient?"

"If you sorely disapprove, I will retrieve whatever volumes you wish. However, without direction, I have brought you my favorites."

She wrestled between being touched by this gesture and thinking it another sign of his controlling nature.

"Aha, and so they must be of the utmost quality if you like them?"

"On the contrary, my favor usually goes against critics. I have chosen from my favorite works based on what Georgiana has told me of you. They were chosen because I believe you'll enjoy them immensely. Worst-case scenario, I figure, it would be an interesting debate to have with you at a later time if you despise my taste."

"Deal," said Elizabeth, amused at glimpsing this new side of him that she hoped (for Georgiana's sake) there was more to.

He stood there for a long while as though working up the courage to say something else, but thought better of it, saying finally:

"I must be off. My household is at your every service, Miss Bennet. I will see you soon."

He left her, then, to choose from the pile of books and to wonder at what he had chosen not to say.

Chapter 10

The three girls, after receiving confirmation that Wickham was aboard a ship to Australia and multiple letters from Mrs. Forster and Mrs. Bennet confirming that the cover-up had gone over without question, enjoyed the grounds of Pemberley together as had not been done in ages (according to housekeeper, Mrs. Reynolds). When, in two weeks, they were invited to the Darcy's townhome in London with the gentleman, there were serious concerns about leaving.

"My brother certainly knows how to pose an argument, he enclosed an invitation to dine with my dearest aunt in London as well as the schedule of the opera house. Not to mention we shall just make it in time for the McCorman's Ball which my brother has promised to take me to now that I sit on the eve of being of the age. He must be truly desperate to have us follow him."

"We will follow you anywhere," said Lydia, for once enjoying her time in the quiet country so much that the mention of a large, private ball only gave her eyes the faintest light.

"Well, it is just that I have spent the loveliest past few weeks here."

"As the company would not change with the setting, I believe we would have just as much fun there as here, Anna."

"Anna" was the nickname that Lydia gave Georgiana once she had deemed "Georgie" reserved for her brother and Colonel Fitzwilliam. "Anna," she had said, "has a stately air…you are no doubt known amongst the *ton* as Georgiana, this will add a sense of mystery to your identity –you will be known to your closest confidantes as *'Anna'* and those not yet close enough to call you that will strive to become friendly enough with you until they are."

"I hope you do not mind my sister's fantastical air," Elizabeth had said once Lydia had finished her speech.

"Not at all," Georgiana had laughed. "I quite like my nickname. My mother's name was 'Anne,' and so it is nice to hear it when referring to me. My brother, I think, will like it."

"London or Pemberley has no bearing on me," said Elizabeth. "I can enjoy myself anywhere."

"Is not Jane in London with our Aunt?" Lydia piped up.

"Which sister?" Georgiana asked excitedly, having heard all about them.

"Jane, the eldest," said Lydia. "She and Elizabeth are our aunt's favorites."

"I would not say that," Elizabeth said. "It is simply that Jane and I have spent the most time with her, before she had children of her own."

"I see," said Georgiana. "Well, if we should go to London, I insist that you and Lydia stay at our townhome and, if she would be so willing, that Jane joins us."

The matter was decided over supper: the girls would indulge the gentlemen and join them in two days time if "balls, shopping, dinner parties, and the theatre were guaranteed," as Lydia worded it.

Chapter 11

"I no longer recognize these expressions as belonging to my sister, Fitzwilliam. It could have been Lydia Bennet who wrote this letter back for all her inferences that they would not join us unless we promised them entertainment." Mr. Darcy fumed, still not sold on the idea of the Georgiana being so close to the Bennets. The elder, surely, was preferable, but he was still confident that he could find her more suitable company amongst the upper classes. At least the young Bennet had calmed rather quickly, considering what she had nearly dragged her family into. Of asking the eldest Bennet to stay with them, Darcy was of the same mind –he didn't know her, and didn't wish to know her.

"She is a young *lady*, Darcy, a *LADY* –the same as you and I dance with on the rare occasion that we leave this stronghold of a townhome of yours."

"You may leave whenever you wish. Might I suggest now?"

"Always letting your temper rule you, cousin. It's a wonder you do not strike me. Did you not mean what you put in your last letter to Georgiana? Do you not wish to take them to dinners, balls, and the theatre?"

"I wrote that by your suggestion, as you well know. Something about making nice or other. I would love to take Georgiana to these things, of course. Her companions are another story."

"You are so quick to judge."

"Have I ever been wrong?"

"You did not have the cleanest betting streak at school, Darce. I wouldn't ask me, if I were you. If you would like to hear about yourself as you would like to be portrayed, ask Bingley. Where is Bingley?"

"He probably doesn't even know, you know him. I will write to him once the ladies are settled here. You think I'm doing the right thing?"

"It was my suggestion, Darcy. It is the least you could do after the way you treated Miss Bennet."

"What would you have done in my position? You are too easily trusting of women, cousin."

"It's usually the other way around," Colonel Fitzwilliam boasted, smirking.

"I don't know what sort of girl Miss Bennet is, I don't know where she comes from, and I don't know anything of her family. If she is the wrong sort of person to be around, then it is..."

"...up to Georgiana to decide," Colonel Fitzwilliam finished decidedly. "She is young, yes. She has made mistakes, yes. But you and I acknowledged our desire that she have more friends of the same age. She is doing *exactly* what we wanted." "I admit, when she wrote to me of having Miss Bennet to Pemberley, I was completely sold on the idea. It was not until this business with Wickham that I began to doubt it because it was only then that I realized that she could be anybody. If her sister was foolish enough to run away with Wickham, then..."

"Careful, Darcy," Fitzwilliam warned. "You cannot say much about that situation without insulting your own sister. You owe it to Georgiana –to yourself, to relax and let others decide matters as befits their own lives. God forbid someone should want what you do not. Let Mr. Bingley be your only puppet."

"What is that supposed to mean?"

"Oh, you know perfectly well what I mean. He would do anything you advise him to do and you do not even take into account his wishes or character before issuing orders. He is off, for instance, God knows where hunting for a country estate under your direction. Did he want a country estate? Who knows? You did not take the time to consult him and he did not bother to ask the question himself."

"I have taken Mr. Bingley under my wing to ensure that he does not waste his father's earnings frivolously. He is the first of his generation out of trade and I afford him my guidance."

"Afford him your guidance? Darcy, he is a grown man. I've heard the two of you, it is not a discussion, it is you making decrees."

"What will you have me do? I cannot seem to have gotten anything right these days! Not with my sister, my friends, my household…did I see to Wickham's deportment alright?"

Colonel Fitzwilliam began to think he had gone too far. What was said needed to be said, but perhaps not all at once. Still, one matter led to another, and he was fairly confident he could end the matter by drawing a comparison between all of his accusations. Worst-case scenario, he would have to sleep at his brother's townhome.

"Remember what I first said, that you let your temper take hold of you? If you calmed enough to listen to reason, you might hear this: you believe yourself to be infallible because it has kept you brave for this long, but you no longer need to attack every instance with this mindset. Georgiana is growing, she's practically a woman, she can and *will* make her own decisions. Bingley, pushover though he may be, can stand to benefit more from your suggestions rather than your commands. He, like Georgiana, is grown and must make decisions based upon his desired future. Miss Bennet and her sister have done nothing but help Georgiana find herself and bring laughter into your home once again. No one —not I, not Georgiana, not the Bennets, not Bingley, will ever be perfect. It is not up to you to try to force your idea of perfection upon any of us. After all —you are not perfect yourself."

"Alright, that is enough of a lecture for one night. Since when did you become all-knowing?"

"Since I drank all of your bourbon."

Chapter 12

Elizabeth took advantage of the rare quiet of the coach ride to London to mull over the events of the past couple of weeks and wonder at what the future would bring. She was happier than she could admit to either Georgiana or her sister to see Jane and hoped that, at least if Mr. Darcy would not allow her to stay, she could make frequent visits.

She was especially eager for Jane to witness the change that had occurred in such a short time in their youngest sister. Silly though she was, it was funneled into a more appropriate way now with the guidance of herself and Georgiana. She no longer had her mother and Kitty to indulge her and allow her to run wild. Kitty would be distressed at the change, Elizabeth knew, but hoped she would adapt to be more like her younger sister for the good of both of them.

It was a secret worry of hers that she and Lydia would be made uncomfortable at Darcy's townhome by the master himself and so would have to depart soon. She had taken the steps necessary in that case and had written to her aunt to warn her of their impending arrival, saying that they were the guests of the Darcy's but hinting that there was no way of knowing for how long. When Elizabeth had gently broached the subject with Georgiana, alluding that she would not be to blame if they were not able to stay, she insisted that Elizabeth was being foolish.

"I am grown," she had said, "he must accept this. I must learn to be hostess, at least, before I shadow Mrs. Reynolds in learning to be a mistress of my own home."

"Why has your brother not married?" Lydia had asked her.

"I have not seen him around many ladies," she said, "but if he acts at all like how he was around the two of you, I think that answers your question."

The conversation had dissolved into a fit of giggles.

Elizabeth was sure that the kind greeting they received from Darcy was all Colonel Fitzwilliam's doing as the host's every move was shadowed by his cousin. Still, the attempt at chivalry both pleased and amused her and she was decidedly relieved on Georgiana's behalf. If she were made uncomfortable in the slightest, Elizabeth would see it necessary to remove herself at once and stay with her Aunt.

"Elizabeth, allow me to show you to the library before you settle in your room, just in case I do not have the opportunity to do so later," said Mr. Darcy, as more of an afterthought. She looked to Colonel Fitzwilliam before consenting, gauging his reaction to the 'off script' way in which Mr. Darcy was conducting himself. Fitzwilliam was worried – there was no doubt of that, but he did not say anything to deter the trip to the library nor attempt to accompany them. And, so, it was with a slightly agitated look on his face, that Darcy led her to a quaint (in respect to the Pemberley library) library tucked away at the back of the house with a two-wall view of the garden with a warm fireplace in between. Elizabeth gasped, delighted.

"You like it?" Darcy asked, because he *had* to say something.

"I adore it, Mr. Darcy. Thank you." It was not as grand as Pemberley's library, but there was something about it that she preferred –though she could not quite put her finger on it. She walked amongst the shelves, letting her fingers run across the back of the volumes as though the only way to choose one was through feeling alone.

"The same rules apply here as did at Pemberley –there are none," said Mr. Darcy watching her from the doorway, perfectly transfixed. "This is your place as much as it is mine, and I expect you here as often as you want."

"I think," Elizabeth said, attempting to verbalize the charm of the place, "that its appeal is a surprise because of its setting. It is an oasis, completely unexpected."

Darcy was lost —he did not think she was speaking specifically to him, but, either way, he was unable to make an answer. He was spellbound, lost in the picture that her words painted for him as she continued. It was as though he was taken back to the first time his father had shown him this library, as though he was seeing it again for the first time but this time, through *her* eyes. She stood in front of him before he realized that she had returned to the doorway. *Her large, beautiful, deep, green eyes...*

"I was quite proud of you today, Darce," said Colonel Fitzwilliam once the gentlemen had separated from the ladies after supper. He did not understand *how* but, *somehow*, he had finally influenced his cousin. Little did he know that it was Elizabeth who was responsible for the change in his behavior. The library had changed everything, and was about to change more. "What have you to say for yourself? You are my cousin still, are you not?"

Darcy was stirred from his dead-end reverie. "I am experimenting with what you have suggested, Fitzwilliam." He could not entirely place the change that had come over him in the library, but he was willing to go along with it until it was understood.

"Oh? And so far, how is it coming along?"

"Miss Bennet, though I am not familiar with her family and upbringing, seems a bright enough girl. I see positive changes in her youngest sister and I have tried to look upon them through the eyes of my sister who is so easily amused by their ramblings. What concerns me is that they are so different from her."

"We sat at the same table this evening, Darcy, and I didn't detect any harmful differences."

"Miss Bennet too easily speaks her mind," the words were out before Darcy could stop them.

"The woman is brilliant. The fastest mind I've ever seen."

Darcy could not bring himself to agree with him. There was something to be mistrusted in a mind made up so quickly. They were fleeting opinions, at most, that she expressed. "Do not be as quick as she to think that. She most likely changes her mind as soon as the statements leave her mouth."

"Or, she has spent all of her young life forming these views…"

"In what setting? The country? What wisdom could be accrued there?"

Fitzwilliam's eyes screamed all he wished to say to his cousin, yet he could not help voicing it as well: "You are a miserable old sod. What the bloody hell happened to you?"

Torn between anger and shame, Darcy made no answer. *I grew up,* he wanted to say, but couldn't bring himself to do so. His cousin left him, then, to join the ladies, saying that he would make the proper excuses if Darcy did not join them in a matter of minutes. Darcy reclined and mulled over the bourbon that his servants had spent the morning replenishing for his cousin's sake.

Darcy *had* changed, certainly –drastically, since the death of his father, since he had been required to step into the position of Master of Pemberley, not an easy task. It was without guidance that he suddenly, a man of nine of twenty, was responsible for everything he had: his estate and his sister. He was Master of over one hundred servants and patrons and both father and mother to a young girl all in a moment. He had to change, he had to harden and, until now, he didn't believe he had gone too far. But now, in the darkness of his study, he couldn't remember the last time he had taken

Georgiana to the sea, played billiards with Fitzwilliam...*laughed*.

When Darcy joined his company a quarter of an hour later, he was too lost in thought to pay the festivities any mind.

Chapter 13

"Brother?" Georgiana's voice cracked as she knocked gingerly on his study door.

"Georgie, what is wrong?" Darcy wrenched the door open more violently than he meant to –a man out of his mind when it came to the well being of his sister. She jumped, realizing what her tone had put him through.

"I'm sorry, Will, I'm sorry! I did not mean to frighten you!" She collapsed in his arms, feeling as helpless as she had when she was a child. Darcy patted her hair and held her tight.

"Sit down, sweetheart. I only thought something was wrong." He began chuckling then, an impulse completely out of his control. Just less than a week ago, he had realized that he hadn't laughed in an age, and there he was, laughing uncontrollably.

"What is it?" Georgiana asked, dumbfounded.

"I can't even begin to explain it, I am so sorry for the sudden change."

"Do not apologize, brother, I haven't seen you smile, let alone laugh, in a very long time." This only spurred his bursts of chuckles. "What did I say?"

When he regained control after a few moments, he tried to put words to what had happened. "It was only that assumed something was wrong –granted, your tone suggested it, but it was only a few days ago that our cousin accused me of jumping to the worst conclusion all the time."

"Oh," Georgiana said, not quite understanding. "I do not think that you do, necessarily."

"I think if you could read my mind...well, I hate to admit when Fitzwilliam is right. And, after that, I realized that

I hadn't laughed in a long while, and the whole circumstance just now became a lot funnier for that reason."

"Why haven't you been happy, brother? That is what I came to talk to you about. Of course nothing has been very easy for you, but I was worried that my entanglement with Wickham prolonged your sadness that just began to subside after our father's death."

"Georgie, it was not you."

"No, I know that now. I knew it all along, in fact. I only needed to voice it and to have it contradicted. Elizabeth told me what I needed to hear. Why are you not happy with her? She is my greatest friend and I cannot even enjoy her company knowing that you…disapprove or something."

Darcy felt like crying then. It was as though she was breathing life into all of his cousin's accusations. How could not justify anything he had done, anything he had said. He had tried –always, and especially after the death of their father, to do the right thing, the noble thing. He had always imagined adult life to be so easy, that everything became black and white once you had grasped the idea of right and wrong in adolescence, but it was so much more complicated than that. It all rested upon his shoulders –all of it. There was no more right and wrong, it was all gray. It was all up to him to sort it, to make the distinction, from his own, grown perspective. And so far, he had made a mess of it. The only thing he was sure that he had done right was extradite Wickham. But that would not have been necessary had he revealed him for what he was in the first place…*then*, he thought, *Elizabeth's lovely eyes would have never been blackened.*

"Elizabeth says that we should only dwell on the past as it gives us pleasure, but to dwell at all denies us the present and risks our future," Georgiana continued. "William, please?"

"I do not even know where to begin, Georgie… Do you mind that Fitzwilliam and I still call you 'Georgie?' I know that Miss Bennet and Miss Lydia call you Anna."

"That is a testament to how little you have been paying attention, William, and how unwilling you have been to ask for help or guidance. I know that you were given an enormous amount of responsibility at a young age that you were less than prepared for —because who could have been prepared to lose a father and a mother, gain a baby sister, three properties, and dozens of servants in a moment? But, what I want you to understand, what I think has been the problem all along —is that you see yourself as doing it alone. I may have not been able to help *then,* but I am *now,* and you need to take advantage of it. You need to include me. If you think you can do everything on your own, well…you'll be forced to in not much time, for no one will be willing to offer assistance. You are too stubborn for your own good, William. You have more sense than most your age and you insist upon sharing it with everyone else, leaving little for yourself!" Georgiana breathed heavily after such a speech and caught her breath before starting up again. "I am your baby sister, William. I always will be. However, I am not a baby any longer. You and Fitzwilliam may call me —*should* call me Georgie forever, for I will always be little to both of you. Lydia has deemed me 'Anna' because she and her sister met me as a young woman…" Darcy hoped she hadn't caught his wince at the term *young woman,* "…as the rest of the world will see me. I like my new nickname, Will. It reminds me of our mother's, Anne, and reminds me that she will always be close by."

"You are the spinning image of her, Georgie. More and more everyday."

They hugged then, a more vulnerable embrace than they had shared in a long while. When they parted, Georgiana cleared his conscience with this:

"I know it has been hard, brother. We need not say more on the subject. Just please —for me, for Fitzwilliam, for *you*: relax. Let others in, hear others' opinions, accept help, ask for it. The greatest people either of us will probably ever meet surround you. Fitzwilliam is the funniest person, Lydia, the most energetic and imaginative, Elizabeth...I cannot even describe her. Why, allow me to let you in one a little secret. At first, when I first began to know her, I almost thought that she'd be perfect for you. I have never met a woman (do not dare discount me for my limited view of the world) so complimentary to you. She is a formidable wit, William, and makes me laugh until I am in tears at least once a day. I have put aside my thoughts of matchmaking because I have no other care in the world but to see you both happy –separately, I mean, I have abandoned the thought that Caroline Bingley holds so dear, that marriage alone brings happiness. In any case, I think Fitzwilliam might try to fight you for her."

The mention of his cousin stirred Darcy from his happy daydream: "Fight me?"

"Yes. If I did not know better, I'd think that he liked Elizabeth," Georgiana related.

"The second son of an earl cannot marry where there is not a dowry," Darcy said, more harshly than he meant to.

"Relax, brother. It may only be a fleeting fancy. In any case, I know nothing of the Bennet girls' dowries, neither does Fitzwilliam. But this is all useless talk, Elizabeth would not marry him for anything."

"No?"

"No. She has told me that she could not be persuaded into matrimony apart from the promise of the deepest love and most genuine, shared affection which she always shared that she was not sure existed."

"Rather overly romantic, don't you think?"

"Not if it exists, no."

Chapter 14

Elizabeth could not say for certain what had come over Mr. Darcy, but something had caused a change in him, and, mostly for Georgiana's sake, she was pleased. He was nearly the brother she had heard so much about before meeting what was once a stale, brooding figure. A week after they had come to London, Mr. Darcy spoke his mind not only when it was to belittle; he engaged, listened to his sister, cousin, and guests, and even, on occasion, laughed.

"What is the status of your sister, Miss Bennet?" Darcy asked on the first occasion they were allowed one corner of the sitting room to themselves. "Your elder sister, I meant, I can see for myself that Miss Lydia is perfectly well."

He smiled, the action accentuating his large eyes. He was letting his stubble form into a slip of a beard that Elizabeth felt tempted to tell him would look attractive. Somehow he looked too stern clean-shaven, or at least the scruffy stubble humanized him and made him more approachable. Either way, the way his eyes drew her in was undeniable. It had frustrated her when, at first, he had been so off-putting because it shouldn't be possible that someone with such deep, alluring eyes could be so cruel. The Darcy she had come to get used to the past few days, however, suggested to her that there was far more to the gentleman than she previously thought.

"Lydia is doing remarkably well, Mr. Darcy, and I have you and your family to thank. It is the cheerful and supportive environment that you have helped to create that has made it possible. My parents will not recognize her when she comes home."

"Is she so changed?"

"She is so *grown*. As for our eldest sister, Jane, I made plans to visit her on the morrow but we have not gone beyond that."

"My sister would enjoy her company here if your aunt and uncle can spare her."

Elizabeth hid her smile —she knew, she did not know how, but she knew, that he was not yet ready to express his own kind feelings and so extended them in the guise of their belonging to others.

"I am well aware of your sister's opinion. What of yours?"

Darcy, as always, was taken aback by her forwardness. There was nothing he could do, he felt, to hide from her perceptive eyes. It was exhausting, operating under her gaze. Yet, all he wanted was her approval: to rise to the challenge.

"I have a feeling I will not get to know one Bennet very well until I get to know them all," he said, not wishing his joke to be perceived as a stab at flirting.

Greater relief than he expected came when Elizabeth let out a hearty laugh, ones that he had only heard sparingly and usually after something amusing that his cousin had said. He kept his gaze purposefully away from his cousin, not wishing to see if he was watching them.

"You, poor soul, have no idea what you are saying. If you stand Jane, myself, and Lydia all under one roof, you are a strong man; but to include my mother and two sisters, well…then you'd be a crazy man. And now you've made me miss my poor father." Her lighthearted titters were so genuine that Darcy joined in her laughter.

"I'm helplessly curious now," he said, hoping he was getting the hang of teasing her if it would produce more reactions like this.

"Then let us hope my father never hears of it, for he will worry that his daughters have spent so much time with one so foolish."

"Let him hear, I would enjoy surprising him."

"Let us see...you would be challenged at cards, chess, literary theory, history...you better study."

"Have you ever bested your father at chess?"

"I have. Only once."

"Then might you spare an hour playing with me? If I lose, perhaps I will reconsider the *great Bennet Invitational*."

Elizabeth laughed in a way he had never heard or seen of her before. Her eyes squinted as she nearly roared, as though shocked that he had said such a thing. She was, in fact, more than surprised at the change in him and impressed that his joke had struck her as so hilarious.

"Well now there's so much more going into it than it just being a game, Mr. Darcy. I accept. I have never been one to back down from a challenge and I feel confident assuming the same of you."

Their game lasted longer than even the others were willing to stay up, but this hardly went noticed by the participants. Elizabeth was proud to say that they were pretty evenly matched though she did not wish to learn Darcy's opinion. It was not until they were alone until they began to converse. First, about nothing in particular, until Darcy brought up the stack of books he had brought her.

"I don't know how much longer you intended me to wait, but I can stand it no longer. How did you find the books I gave you?"

She eyed him with a quizzical look, wondering how much teasing she could get away with.

"If you mean to distract me by beginning what will surely become a philosophical conversation concerning poetry and literature, then you must meet my father —I could converse about Byron in my sleep."

"Is that why you are so opinionated? I imagine from the sound of things that you take after your father more than your mother."

"Of his daughters, I take after my father most, yes. He has spent more time held up in his study than he has anywhere else and since I insisted on joining him for the better part of my childhood, he thought it was worthwhile to instruct me. I do not think I am more opinionated than any other person, I just find that I express it more readily and more often."

In this very moment, Darcy was convinced that (man or woman), Miss Bennet was the most interesting person he had ever met. But even this realization could not be used an excuse for losing miserably to her in chess an hour later. This loss did, however, add to his esteem of her, as did her opinion of his favorite books. If she liked a passage or volume, she had an informed reason for it and provided examples different or similar from other works. If she hated it, she had even more reasons for feeling so.

He needed to drastically improve his conversation skills, he realized, this was no woman of the *ton*. Never once did they discuss weather, room décor…and, even then, though their conversation was more on par with what he would deliberated over with a man, she was more informed than most he had before met.

He was asleep that night before his head hit the pillow, leaving no time to even consider the woman that had so exhausted him.

Chapter 15

"Aha, I see that my cousin is afraid to show his face?" Colonel Fitzwilliam said to Elizabeth once he had arisen to see that Mr. Darcy was not yet up.

"I cannot say if that has anything to do with it."

"But you did win, eh? That's good! I'd say that a bit of humbling would do him good, but it's not like it's a surprising loss, Miss Bennet. I would have bet a year's salary on you."

"Thank you, Colonel, but I would never have allowed that."

"I assure you, you would never have known. But you would have received an anonymous gift, in any case, for making a kind man a fortune."

"My brother was a good sport, was he not?" asked Georgiana, suddenly realizing what behavior her brother was capable of if he were in a bad mood.

"He was the perfect gentleman, I assure you," Elizabeth answered once Colonel Fitzwilliam had ceased his impression of his cousin losing at chess. "The game was a lengthy one, it does not surprise me that he is still abed, it was not easy for me to get up this morning."

"I am amazed that you are such a consistently early riser, Miss Bennet," said Colonel Fitzwilliam just as Mr. Darcy and Lydia joined them. "Ah, there are the bed bugs."

Elizabeth smiled, gladdened by Colonel Fitzwilliam's attentions to Lydia. It was helpful, no doubt, to have her amongst such admirable male company. He teased her just as much as he teased Georgiana and this she found very humorous.

"If I look like a bug, Colonel, I'm marching right back to bed for there is no reason for me to be up and about, worrying about the day," Lydia said, giggling. She was coming into her own more and more each day, picking out qualities she liked in each of the elders surrounding her before trying those traits on for herself. She was all that a wonderful girl could be: playful, attentive, energetic, kind –but all these had been lost or masked amongst her inappropriate behavior. She had recently come to channel them and was becoming a true and beautiful person.

"A LADYBUG, Miss Lydia, a *lady*bug!" Fitzwilliam cried. "A garden fairy, as Darcy and I used to call them for Georgiana." They all laughed, none more than Elizabeth, who was enjoying both Fitzwilliam's save as well as imagining Darcy saying 'garden fairy.'

"Well, Mr. Darcy," Lydia said, "shall we tend to the flowers?"

"I suppose it is our duty, Miss Lydia. Do the ladybugs require other company? Or should we leave them to their laughter?"

Lydia consented to inviting the entire party, and all went out into the garden for a short morning walk in the garden. Elizabeth hung back with Georgiana, content to watch Lydia converse between Mr. Darcy and Colonel Fitzwilliam. It was the best thing for her, in Elizabeth's opinion, to get a view of men other than as fathers or prospective husbands. The only man she had ever known well was their father and the only other men she knew of were ones she was brought up to believe needed chasing.

Elizabeth wished, in that moment more than any other that they had grown up with brothers. Besides losing their house to the next male kin, as Longbourn was not tailored to fall to the female line, it would have meant more rounded social education. Elizabeth was perhaps the most potentially acclimated to society of all the Bennet sisters. Jane was shy,

Mary, unrelenting, and Kitty and Lydia, far too boisterous. Elizabeth wished that Jane would not be made too uncomfortable in the near constant presence of two gentlemen, for Elizabeth believed it would do a great deal of good. Their mother had scared Jane into believing that she needed to behave a certain way and, so far, she had –but often against her own will. In an uncertain situation without their mother, Jane might flourish.

"Elizabeth, Lydia!" their aunt, Mrs. Gardiner yelled, embracing them. Jane followed her, just as excited and warm, but in her own way. "Oh, look!" Mrs. Gardiner said, holding Lydia's face between her hands. "How you've grown! What a lucky woman I am, to have three nieces under my roof. Lydia, but you are *grown*!"

It was difficult to tell whose smile was larger at the compliment: Elizabeth or Lydia. Elizabeth would have argued that her smile was larger, for it was for her Aunt's sake and Lydia's. Jane agreed that Lydia had quite changed and searched Elizabeth's face for an answer. Elizabeth could do nothing to indulge her –not now or ever. There was no admitting the story about Wickham to anyone but once Jane was introduced to the environment in which they had spent the past few weeks, she would most likely credit that with Lydia's sudden maturation.

They talked for a long while, first of how they had come to meet, a story that Elizabeth and Lydia had practiced on the way over, and then of Elizabeth's stay at Pemberley of which was a source of great interest to her aunt.

"I lived but three miles from that great house and, you know, I never toured it! I have promised myself every spring since that your uncle and I would stop in on our sojourn to the lakes, but we have always run late and not made it in time."

Elizabeth assured her aunt that when she did get the chance to go, that it would not disappoint her. She described the house in such great detail and cleverly (at least she thought) left out all particulars of its master —but this did not go unnoticed by Mrs. Gardiner.

"Of Miss Darcy, I know, of course —so what of Mr. Darcy!"

Elizabeth took a moment to gather her thoughts on the gentleman in question until she was confident in having a full thought to express, but Lydia beat her to it.

"Mr. Darcy is a fine gentleman, Aunt. He and his cousin, Colonel Fitzwilliam, are excellent company. They are a riot together, though Mr. Darcy is shy, a bit like his younger sister, before you get to know him. I used to think he was rather grave because he rarely smiles, but he is very kind."

"Elizabeth?" her Aunt asked, wanting to know if what Lydia had expressed was true. Elizabeth readily agreed before forming an opinion of her own completely, not wishing to give off the impression that she did not like the man. She considered Lydia's words carefully as the ladies continued to discuss the Darcy townhome and whether or not there would be room for Jane. Elizabeth had never before thought of Darcy as *shy. Could Lydia be right?* Georgiana was shy, certainly, but it was a trait more easily hidden on a man, Elizabeth owned, especially one of his status. Either way, it was her turn to express that there was absolutely enough room for Jane and that it would be excellent if she joined the party, assuming their aunt could spare her and with the promise that they'd visit regularly.

"Of course, don't be surprised at receiving invitations to dine with us as well," said Lydia. Elizabeth wondered if Darcy would have a problem inviting the Gardiners to dine with them. After all, this was no longer the country, social etiquette meant a lot more in town and the Gardiners were in trade. She hoped that it would be so, but knew not to be disappointed if it did not come to pass.

All in all, the visit lasted nearly above three hours and the ladies parted with the understanding that Jane would join them in three days time.

Chapter 16

The whole of the townhome was waiting for Elizabeth and Lydia's return and Mr. Darcy, Elizabeth noticed, was scarcely less eager to see them than was his sister. Georgiana nearly jumped up and down when Lydia delivered the news that Jane would be joining them and passed along her sincerest thanks for the hospitality.

"We have just been discussing it amongst ourselves," Georgiana said, "and think it would be marvelous if your aunt and uncle accompany her over and stay for supper."

Elizabeth hid her surprise at the invitation and studied Darcy's face in an attempt to learn his opinion. She saw nothing there but genuine, though concealed kindness, and, when his eyes met hers, smiled at him openly for the first time.

The remainder of the day was spent in the music room where the ladies practiced Darcy's favorite song as a "triplet" where they each were given a part, recognizing that it would need to be expanded into a "quartet" once Jane arrived.
"I am hoping to convince my brother to return us to Pemberley once we have seen to all the shopping, balls, and shows that town has to offer. What do you think?"

"You two are our hosts, we'd follow you anywhere, Georgiana. I have never spent much time in town. All in all, I'd have to say that I belong more in the country."

"I thought so," Georgiana said, "and I know Lydia is more inclined towards the city, am I correct?"

"I would have agreed with you wholeheartedly a matter of weeks ago but now, I find myself happy in both environments. Surely if we attend balls, dinners, shows, and whatever else the city has to offer, I will begin to grow homesick for the sight of trees and grass. I think your idea is a perfect compromise."

Elizabeth and Lydia helped Georgiana as much as they could in the planning of supper for the Gardiners, which the lady insisted, "must be perfect." She had ordered based on Elizabeth's recommendations of the Gardiners' and Jane's favorite foods and had Earl Grey tea prepared for alongside dessert for their aunt, bourbon for their uncle.

"Men are so easily pleased," Georgiana said. "I don't even know why I bother to ask. It is always 'bourbon.' And even when it's not bourbon –it's whiskey or some other dark drink that they can barely tell the difference between in any case. Give a man a strong drink, and he will be happy. Women are far more particular. William's friend's sister, for example, must have her English breakfast tea at night with one spoon of sugar. In the morning, she must have dandelion tea with cream and two spoons of sugar. Unless it is raining, then she insists upon having peppermint tea. The household is in an immediate uproar as soon as she enters our home."

"She sounds like a nightmare," Lydia said bluntly, making Georgiana giggle hysterically.

"I have often called her that in my head and am constantly grateful I am not on the receiving end of her criticism, though I've had to watch poor Mrs. Reynolds be lectured on the average temperature of tea served in London enough time as it is."

"How is her brother?" Elizabeth was curious to find out.

"The picture of kindness, the most easy going man I have ever met. He and my brother studied at university together and, thankfully, he is the polar opposite of his sister, though they travel together almost exclusively. He is the type that would not even require bourbon, for example. You'd have met the both of them already, except that they are touring the countryside on my brother's suggestion that he find a country estate."

Elizabeth found it humorous that two people would do something specifically under Darcy's counsel, and was curious to meet this gentleman if he should ever return from his task. He sounded already, though she of course wished to be contradicted, like a bit of a pushover, but she'd have to meet him to be sure. It would be fitting, however, for someone like that to have an overbearing and critical sister in that he would constantly be bossed around on all sides. Elizabeth was full of pity for the stranger already.

"You should take leave, Fitzwilliam, and accept the help your father has extended to you," Darcy was saying as the ladies entered the dining room.

"I *should* have done and *should* do a lot of things, Darcy. You may offer your advice in the form of an opinion, not as a doctrine."

The argument did not cease, not even after pleasantries were exchanged and all Elizabeth could do was wonder at the coincidence of their conversation. Her head jolted up from her cold soup when her name was mentioned, however, and she dreaded being pulled into the conversation.

"What Miss Bennet said of the subject is the advice I'd like to follow."

Elizabeth had no clue as to what they were discussing and was sure that Colonel Fitzwilliam had never brought it up with her. She racked her brain, determined to recall what he could possibly be referring to.

"And what, Miss Bennet, was your advice?" Darcy said, more challenging than curious.

Colonel Fitzwilliam jumped in then, realizing his error. "Oh, she probably doesn't remember, it wasn't in this context, poor lady. It was," he explained to Elizabeth, "something like, follow your happiness…"

"Oh," Elizabeth said, chuckling, despite the situation, "I remember, though I think we will have to settle for a paraphrasing."

Darcy, despite his mood, found himself enraptured by her modesty and hung on her every word, every movement of her lips...

"It was something like, follow your own happiness, let others guide you when you wish it, but never steer away for long from your own desires. Others cannot tell you what you want, but they can sometimes aid you in getting what you do. Pursue your passion, and happiness will follow –how could you be wrong about you?"

These last words struck Darcy particularly hard and he nearly volunteered an example of how you could be wrong about yourself. After all, he had done many wrongs since assuming his role as Master of Pemberley, his own sister and cousin had found it necessary to point it out to him. Though he did not want to put forward his own specifics, he could not surpass the opportunity to hear what Elizabeth would say of it.

"And what if someone is blinded by their own ignorance, stupidity..." he began.

"Arrogance?" Elizabeth finished.

"Yes," he half-growled, noticing that when Elizabeth spoke to him, it was as though there was no one else in the room. In truth, she felt the same, but she credited it to her concentration on the present subject and he, to something else entirely.

"How could the same not apply? I think, even taking into account this person's arrogance, ignorance, and stupidity, that they are able to recognize that they're unhappy. They just would require more assistance, perhaps, and if they are made to see reason, they are again able to work towards their own contentment. But there, I think, is no heavy-handed direction necessary." She wanted to hear him defend his tendency towards controlling those around him. She was sure that he was the unhappy person he had been referring to but still did not understand why a person admitting to being unhappy would so easily issue advice to others.

"If a friend thinks they know best, would you not want them to share their opinion?"

"Opinions are always welcome, especially from those one holds in the highest esteem. But one cannot issue advice, I think, without first determining what that person wants. If Lydia were to always wish to run away with the circus, I might make better use of my time ensuring that she found appointment with the circus safely rather than trying to talk her out of it. That example is extreme, I own," Elizabeth said above the laughter of the listeners, "but it is to illustrate my point."

"But a girl like Lydia does not belong in the circus, she is meant for better, surely," Darcy said, continuing the metaphor completely straight-faced.

"If I love her, if I truly *love her*, and it is not a passing fancy, then I, who loves her, has the least right to try and stop her. She is meant for what she wants, when she is educated and old enough to choose for herself. To direct her where she does not wish to go will end up making her unhappy and it will cause a rift between us. She will learn to resent me, knowing that I advised her against chasing her dreams."

"That makes sense, Miss Bennet. But it is an extreme sort of example."

"It is an extreme example of what unconditional love means, perhaps the most difficult thing in the world to explain, and even more difficult to put into practice."

"Though you explain it so well, I am reluctant to say that I believe in such a thing."

"As I am, at times. But that does not mean that I shouldn't strive for it. Colonel Fitzwilliam," she said, drawing him back into the conversation, "you are a grown man who can voice what he wants and allow others to guide him towards that. I have no doubt about you being impenetrable to others' whims, not even my own. You are obviously happy, or are on your way to it, I can see it in your eyes."

Colonel Fitzwilliam beamed. "I believe you are correct, madam. Thank you."

She noticed Darcy's piercing stare and wondered what he was thinking. She found that she was reflecting over his opinion a lot these days as he seldom spoke it. His eyes gave little away when he wasn't angry and she did not yet know him well enough to guess. When they had first met, she thought that his dark stare was a physical reflection of his constant displeasure, but since he had warmed up to her (or seemed to at least), she hoped that it was at least no longer the case or that she had been wrong all along.

"I'd marry her if I had a fortune, Darcy. It is not passion that I am overwhelmed by, it is esteem. I have never met a woman who has combined sense, wit, and modesty. She is the most beautiful person I have ever met." Colonel Fitzwilliam downed the rest of his bourbon glass in Elizabeth's honor, adding that he hoped the eldest Bennet was not half so impressive otherwise he'd lose his mind. "But what do you think, now that you have spent more time with her? Tell me you see all that has captured me?"

Darcy could not bring himself to voice an opinion that was his own, mostly because he had not designated his yet. He was, if he were truthful, on the precipice of saying something either far too kind or far too mean. "I do not disagree with you, Fitzwilliam, she possesses all the qualities that you have described." This was the best possible answer he could give, he surmised, for it was vague but sociable.

"You are not romantic in the least, Darce! Tell me she has not in the least bit touched your heart? It must be made of stone is she has not!"

"Romance? You have not mentioned your heart, Richard; you have left out any mention of 'love.' You *esteem* her —you *respect* her —she *interests* you. But she has not captured your heart in the least, your head at most."

"Maybe you are romantic after all…"

"Call me what you will, but if you should speak of having money for the sole purpose of marrying someone you are not madly in love with…then…"

"So you —Darcy of Pemberley, who has more money that most barons and sirs and kings —you plan to, with all of your riches, marry for love? Is that what you're telling me? Ignoring title, ignoring propriety, ignoring age, beauty, education…love is what will land a lady the title of Mistress of Pemberley?"

"I was not talking about *my* standing, I was discussing yours."

"Well *now* we are discussing *yours*. You have said that if I wish for money it should be in the event that I am completely enraptured. So, seeing how you have given this advice so effortlessly and that you *have* money, is that what you plan to do?"

"To explain what I have said using Miss Bennet's words, I simply was advising you based on what I know of your own desires. You are more romantic than I. If you wish to have money in order that you may marry, you might as well do so when you are completely lost in love. You must be the more romantic of the two of us."

"That is where you're wrong, cousin. I have found love plenty of times. Often between my sheets, both alone and with company."

"That is foul."

"But true. I have stolen kisses, I have stolen hearts, given mine away a few times. Lost sleep over ladies I have only glimpsed in the street. Spent many an hour wondering what it would have been like, what we would have been like, together… But, I am resigned to my place in the world. I have not fallen so hard that I am not able to pick myself back up. I am at liberty to fall in love as many times as it is possible for me to do so and still hold old for a woman of title, consequence, and wealth to be Mrs. Fitzwilliam. You —who clings to celibacy, is the more romantic of us, though it is only I that celebrates matters of the heart and mind."

"Heart or loins?"

"I would say both, though you could never be persuaded until you lived and loved as I have. I have a feeling that the lucky lady I end up with will be utterly unrecognizable in comparison to the women I have spent my time with leading up to her. She will be new, interesting, and the last love of my life because my past will have designated it so."

"Then we do disagree. But I do remember quite a different man —oh, seven summers ago? Quite a whimsical poet when it came to matters of the heart. And even then, his idea of love, in the context of marriage, was still built upon mutual respect, an equality of class, and a similar upbringing."

"That was a boy. A man has taken his place," Fitzwilliam answered abruptly. "Opposites attract, Darcy. They say that your soul mate will be all to you where you fall short."

"I think that a soul mate is one that builds upon your strengths to make them stronger."

"We disagree again. You cannot hope to be passionate about all whom you esteem, any that you are equal to in rank that grew up as practically your own sister has. You *must be* looking for someone different —otherwise you would have found her already. You would have married one of these stiff backed, rigid-necked, pompous buffoons of the *ton* with their designer dresses, pressed hair, and delicate sensibilities. In other words, you: in female form."

"Very amusing," was all Darcy could say, not wishing to discredit his cousin and add more fuel to his fire. He was right, he thought, in one respect. If the lady he wished to marry was a lady he had described...surely he would have met her already.

"I will discontinue my quest for a pot of gold to marry Miss Bennet and resolve to continue my life as I know it must be. But I urge you to think better on what you want. You have always had structure, normality. I am no stranger to passion and I suggest you include that in your list of requirements for a wife."

They joined the ladies then and were treated to a rendition of Darcy's favorite song as performed by all three girls, together at some parts, separate at others. Darcy heard the words as never before, gleaning an entirely new meaning from them. It was a love song, as most were, but he had never before heard the sadness behind the lyrics hidden beneath the upbeat rhythm of the piano score. It ended happily, but Darcy could not shake the feeling that the middle of the song had given to him. It was the part that Elizabeth had sung: the lyrics had described being "wrong in love," in being so close to missing what was right in front of whomever had written it and nearly missing the love of their life altogether. But by the end, Georgiana's part, the singer had righted his wrongs and claimed his love, and celebrated owning to his mistakes and, more than that, having been strong enough to correct them.

"I like the music well enough," Elizabeth was saying by the time Darcy was able to pay attention to his surroundings once again. "But I do not know if I could sympathize with a man who was being such a dolt." Georgiana and Kitty were laughing before Colonel Fitzwilliam's booming chuckle joined in.

"Is not righting your wrongs an admirable quality, Miss Bennet?" Darcy interrupted, too serious to match their gaiety.

"It is, but so is being right in the first place. Society is often too preoccupied with rewarding those who have blundered and corrected, rather than those who have had the foresight and intellect to stay on the path of righteousness all along."

He took offense, he realized, as though she were directing her comment at him. He schooled his irrational anger before answering, saying:

"Perhaps neither should be held above the other or it should at least be considered at a case by case basis."

"I cannot disagree with that."

"You are too romantic for this song, I think," chimed in Lydia to her sister.

"No doubt my Prince Charming will ride up on his white horse and manage no mistakes, Lydia, you are correct, I am too romantic." Everyone laughed except Darcy, who felt more dour than ever, though he could not say why.

"If he and I should meet, I will point him in your direction, Miss Bennet," said Colonel Fitzwilliam. "Darcy, I'm in the market for a white horse, let me know if you're aware of any sellers." Everyone burst into laughter and Elizabeth had to wipe hysterical tears from her face. Her favorite sense of humor was the kind that was unexpected, and this slight breech of impropriety certainly fit the bill.

"You could always dye yours," suggested Lydia.

"A novel idea, young Bennet! For if I am to pretend to be a charming prince, I could also get away with riding a dyed horse. Something tells me that I will not get help from my cousin in this endeavor," he said, throwing a glance at Darcy who had been frowning openly since the subject was broached.

"No, I cannot condone nor assist in deceiving a young lady."

"You are *too* serious, brother!" Georgiana chided him. "We could put an ad in the paper, Lizzy," she said, at last having the courage to call Elizabeth by the nickname that she had so often heard Lydia use.

"Wanted: handsome prince, white horse," began Elizabeth, "well mannered, filthy rich, well educated but not pompous..."

"Manly," Lydia added, "chivalrous, with good taste in ribbons, jewelry, and wine..."

"With a perfect sense of humor, a tendency towards laughter, plenty of friends, the dream host, and a hopeless romantic," finished Georgiana.

"Now that we know what to look for in a horse, what of your handsome prince?" asked Colonel Fitzwilliam to the uproar of his audience, even Darcy cracked a smile. "I'm thoroughly intimidated by being let into the minds of the female, ladies. As I'm sure Darcy is also. I'm glad that I am accustomed to bachelorhood, otherwise I might have been disappointed knowing I don't have a shot in hell." Darcy finally found reason to laugh and joined in with the others before clamming up again when Richard continued. "We should at least, Darcy, give them a summary on what we look for. Just to even the stakes. Then we may all wallow in the light of the fire at our lonely lives –together."

Elizabeth was convinced that there was nothing that Fitzwilliam could not make sound funny and she admittedly was excited to hear what he admired in a woman.

"Very well, cousin. If any two men needed to boil it down to a list, I think we are perfectly capable as we tend to be opposites," began Darcy. "She must be well read..."

"Beautiful."

"A tremendous hostess."

"Wealthy."

"Intelligent."

"Confident."

"Active, polite..."

"Feminine and beautiful."

"Yes, beautiful twice," laughed Darcy. "Demur..."

"Funny," Colonel Fitzwilliam stressed. "Teasing."

"I can't think of anything else," Darcy admitted.

"Men are a simple breed. Ironic that we won't find this lady," Richard mused.

"We shall settle for a woman named brandy, and the fine company of these ladies so long as they are here awaiting the arrival of their princes."

"Then we shall *settle* for your company for the present," Lydia teased, "while we wait."

Chapter 17

"Miss Bennet, allow me to start off by explaining that you have made this a very uncomfortable situation for cousin and myself," said Richard to Jane upon her arrival. "Mr. Gardiner, surely you will agree with me that your nieces are amongst the finest women in all of England. Besides your beautiful wife and my wonderful cousin, I do not know what I will do for company afterwards. They dull every other prospect!"

Jane was at a complete loss as to how to react, seeing as she had never before been faced with such impertinence mixed with cordiality. Her silence went unnoticed, however, amongst the resounding laughter that accompanied this, especially from her Aunt and Uncle Gardiner. The gracious couple had no idea what to expect when they arrived on the Darcy's townhome doorstep with their niece, but whatever picture they had held in their mind prior was nothing to the joviality that greeted them. Their laughter was due to a mixture of surprise and genuine enjoyment.

"Well then you understand why I surround myself solely with them, Mr..." Mr. Gardiner trailed off there, realizing he did not know the gentleman's name, only that he could not be Mr. Darcy as he had designated already that Miss Darcy was his niece.

"...Colonel Richard Fitzwilliam, at your service," Richard finished for him, bowing and smiling.

"Colonel, it is a pleasure to make your acquaintance."

"My cousin had to join the military, you see, in order to get away with the sort of behavior he has just shown," said Mr. Darcy from his cousin's side. His was the perfect manner to make the sort of jokes that Elizabeth and the Gardiners found most amusing, for there was nothing in his air or tone that suggested he was joking. This characteristic drew out the surprise and, therefore, the laughs. Colonel Fitzwilliam, always the first to laugh, erupted and the enjoyment grew until it rang louder in the front hall than the response to his initial crack.

It was said that night by all manner of servants that the supper discussion flowed so easily and boisterously that it was as if all at the table were the oldest of friends. Elizabeth barely had time to consider that she had never seen any of her family members so happy, Georgiana ever so at ease, Darcy so open and relaxed. Colonel Fitzwilliam was perfectly in his element, comfortable anywhere, more so if those around him were as content as he. Jane was certainly welcomed into their home and the Gardiners scarcely wished to leave it. Elizabeth was touched when Darcy spoke so eloquently of the town of Lambton where Mrs. Gardiner had grown up and ever so graciously thanked her for the compliment of always wishing to have toured his home.

"It is unfortunate that you did not venture to Pemberley in my father's lifetime, for he often overtook and led the tour himself," explained Georgiana. Did you ever have the chance to meet him?"

Elizabeth had seen from the start of her family's visit that the mistress within Georgiana had finally the occasion to come out. She was gracious, kind, attentive, and would always interject when the conversation needed it, adding helpful comments here and there, asking polite questions when it would move things along. It was the Georgiana that Elizabeth had always seen –but the one that so often hid behind the girlish identity that had been forced upon her by her brother. After tonight, Elizabeth thought, Georgiana the Lady would never retreat again.

"I did not have that honor, dear Miss Darcy. Though I am fortunate enough to say that I was acquainted with your mother."

"Really?" both Georgiana and Darcy said in unison.

Beyond what he had already gleaned of the Gardiners, Mr. Darcy had ample reason to be impressed further. It particularly irked him when someone, especially of the lower classes, insisted upon gaining an acquaintance based upon a mutual one, alone. It was polite, he was always taught, to have made the introduction on one's own merit and wait until the subject arose. Mrs. Gardiner and her husband were not the sort of people that were self-deprecating enough to find the need to claw their way up the social ladder by any means necessary. Caroline Bingley's face, the sister of his good friend, Charles Bingley, swam into view at this thought. The Gardiners, on the other hand, were the sort of people who were grand on their own scale and somehow more entertaining than anyone he had ever before met. He had attended not one social dinner that had included half as much laughter. Everyone in attendance was always too busy thinking about what they should say and how they should act to relax and be themselves within the constraints of propriety. It was too bad, really, he thought, that he would not run into the Gardiners at his Aunt's gatherings or at any balls to which he was invited. But he was having too much fun, for once in his life, for this to have a complete affect on him. He would do what he could to include them and they would never take advantage of his kindness, he knew, as Miss Bingley often did.

"Anne and I met at a small gathering of ladies who had formed a book club in Lambton. Oh, it was such an age ago, but I do remember that your mother and I sat together and I found her to be exactly what I expected from the Mistress of Pemberley. She was beautiful, kind, gracious, and had a rather wicked sense of humor that further complimented these qualities. I did not see much of her, as she was busy at home raising an active young boy, but what I did see of her, I adored. You look exactly like her, Miss Darcy, if I may say so. Particularly when you smile." Georgiana was smiling now, and her smile had never been bigger.

"If you should find yourself en route to the lakes when we are at home," Darcy started in, "you must make a stop. Georgiana and I would be honored to open our home to you."

"Mr. Darcy," Mr. Gardiner breathed, "you are too kind!"

Elizabeth was at a loss for not only words –but also feelings. She was seated across from a stranger this evening, for this Mr. Darcy was an entirely different man than he was just hours before. Of course she could easily give credit to how genuine her aunt and uncle were, but she would not have guessed that they're being kind or not would have any affect on their host. He seemed, until now, untouchable –so walled in by his own design. *Could this be the <u>actual</u> Mr. Darcy? Could the Gardiners have convinced him to let down his guard?*

Even if she had asked the gentleman directly, Darcy could not possibly have answered her, as he could not explain the situation himself. He did not know what had come over him, but he *knew,* he was *sure* –that he would regret nothing of what he had said or done so far that night. It was, as though, somehow –the goodness of these people had put to rest something inside of him that had overwhelmed him thus far, that had inhibited him. He felt remarkable and suddenly wished that he could have been this way since assuming his master-role. *Things would have been so different...*

"We had hoped to be on our way to the lakes as soon as next month, truth be told," Mr. Gardiner said. "We will certainly accept your hospitality the next time, as I am sure you will not be home again so soon. You've only just come into town, am I correct?"

Everyone at the table seemed crestfallen at the news, even Darcy. There was such promise in the idea of having such cheerful people in such a large place. It was as though the idea itself gave way to a thousand more happy possibilities.

"As I certainly did not expect to be in town again so soon, I cannot guarantee that circumstances will not whisk me away back to my home, but it is not our current plan to move so quickly, no. However, in my absence, I will see to it that Mrs. Reynolds knows when to expect you and see to your every comfort." *I cannot stop,* Darcy realized, *being kind. But I don't feel stressed as I normally do —I don't feel it is forced. I feel as I imagine Miss Elizabeth feels when I saw her help the servant that had shattered the teacup all across the floor this morning.* She had gone out of her way, done something unnecessary of her station, but he had never seen anyone so...authentic. It was not for herself that Miss Bennet ever did anything, it was for others. He was beyond grateful that Miss Bingley was not here at the moment, though he could not say precisely why. Something in how she would reacted to his offer, but more in what she would have said of Miss Elizabeth when she left the room to deliver the broken teacup pieces to the kitchen alongside the servant. Now that Mr. Darcy understood how kindness felt —he could not have handled Miss Bingley's criticism.

"Thank you so much, Mr. Darcy," said Mrs. Gardiner. "We shall make sure to set out early enough for such a treat. It'll be the first time we've ever left for that sojourn in a timely manner."

When Mrs. Gardiner had heard that Georgiana had never been to the lakes, Elizabeth thought that her aunt had come rather close to insisting that she join them. "Neither have my nieces!" she mourned. "And it is quite possibly my favorite place in all of Europe."

This began a conversation on where the Gardiners had traveled, quite an extensive list for their class, before having children.

"I do not miss it," Mrs. Gardiner said of staying at home for her children's sake. "Traveling is for the young and, once you've seen what you want and can pick out your favorite place, you will always find the opportunity to go back."

"I'm rather fortunate that our favorite isn't Paris, am I not?" Mr. Gardiner teased. "Can you imagine? All the places we go, and we fall in love with something that's merely hours away by coach?"

"Now you make me absolutely desperate to see it!" Georgiana exclaimed, giggling.

"But seeing the lakes will ruin France, Germany, Italy, and Greece for you!" Richard teased.

"I don't know about that," Mrs. Gardiner said, laughing. "Miss Darcy, you will fall in love with the music that fills all of those places and brings their culture to life."

"I adore music!" Miss Darcy said.

"Music adores *you*," chimed in Lydia. "You should hear her on the piano, Aunt."

"Then you shall love it. Leave an old lady like me to enjoy the silence of the lakes while you explore the sounds of Europe!"

Chapter 18

"Brother," Georgiana said quietly but firmly upon entering his study as soon as the mail arrived the following morning. "I wanted to catch you before breakfast and before your letters give you cause to be distracted."

"Oh?"

"Yes. But I see you've already begun answering correspondence. You and Elizabeth *must* teach me how to read so quickly!" She gestured to the already opened letter and the response he had already begun.

"It is just as your talent at the piano keys, it just takes practice."

"Well then it also takes patience."

"Exactly. You needn't concern yourself about the letter I have already opened as cause for alarm, it is only from Bingley and he can only ever cause a slight headache."

"Well, as soon as I tell you what I am determined to say, I would love to hear about Bingley. Now," she began, clearing her throat, "I quite liked the Gardiners."

"As did I."

"I quite loved their company."

"As did I."

"As I could tell. Now. Promise me you will not speak a word until I have finished –until I give you leave to give me your opinion on *all* that I have said, not only bits and pieces if I am interrupted."

"I promise," he said sternly, more curious than weary.

"If the Bennets' family are able to spare them longer, William, I should very much like to return to Pemberley with them once we have taken in all the sights and sounds of town.

It will be my first ever-real act as mistress and since we left in such a rush I felt there was much more to do. I know you don't particularly like town, so of course I would love it if you joined us. This would put us at home at the same time the Gardiners were en route to the lakes and we would again be rewarded with their company. This brings me to the biggest idea. I should like to form a caravan and accompany them to the lakes with the Bennets. Now, think on it before you agree or disagree, please. And imagine how different and perfect it would be in comparison to what we're used to."

One year ago he could not have brought himself to say "no" to anything that Georgiana asked and now, fully grown, she was even more difficult to deny as she came to make more sense.

"You do not know what a coincidence this is, Georgie."

Georgiana looked up at him, taken aback by this response. There was a hint of hope in her eyes. Hoping for a yes...

"Bingley has just informed me that he will be in the area of Pemberley next month as his country estate tour is ending there. He has planned it that way, he claims, so as to meet us there if we happen to be at home which he says he thinks is likely as I was never one to remain patient in town. I have just been writing to him to explain that we do not yet have plans to return to Pemberley so soon, but now that you have brought this plan to my attention, it is certainly something to consider."

"My, that is a coincidence. I suppose, if the timing was right, they could join us."

"You'd certainly get a good stab at hosting then, it would be a full house." Georgiana paled considerably at this, and so he continued. "I'm sorry, Georgiana, I did not mean to frighten you. These are all your friends, there would be no pressure."

"It is not the Bennets that I am nervous in front of, nor even the Gardiners now, though we have just met. It is Caroline Bingley whom I would rather wish to avoid in such a context."

Oh. Darcy had no concrete response for that. His sister was right, but not wholly...

"If you are fearful of Caroline Bingley, then I should encourage you to face her. But let me say this, if this fear is accompanied by a lack of respect, then I suggest you do away with your trepidation by realizing that if you do like or respect her –then her opinion hardly matters and it is nothing to be fearful of."

Georgiana looked startled at his comment. He had never before said anything so blunt in her presence. He had always tiptoed around criticisms, or so he thought, in order that she be allowed to make her own opinion. In any case, he had once believed that Caroline Bingley's company was preferable to someone like the Bennet girls at one time or another solely based on status. Perhaps that made him no better than the off-putting lady herself...believing that status guaranteed a certain quality of person. In comparing Miss Bingley to the Bennets and the Gardiners (who were, at this moment, of trade), the upper class fell abysmally short.

Georgiana laughed when she realized that her brother was perfectly serious. It was something she expected of Lydia to say. Blunt, honest, and playfully unforgiving.

"But you have always shown her kindness, William. Why, at first, I was afraid that..."

"That I would allow her to sink her claws into me and marry her? Georgiana, listen to me." He bade her sit down and get comfortable. "As you grow older, you come to realize that nothing is as it seems. For example, I grew up thinking that our aunt, Lady Catherine, and mother were the best of friends. Only when she was sick did she confide in me that I needed to be weary of her. She had maintained the relationship for my sake, she said, to keep up the appearance of a happy family and a loving aunt. But, on her deathbed, she warned that this would not continue once she was gone. I could not make sense of what mother told me for a long while afterwards, but she insisted that Lady Catherine had no true motives that could be seen with the naked eye…that she would do anything to see her daughter as the Mistress of Pemberley. Low and behold, she tried to strong arm me into such a union within the a year of our mother's death."

"But you were a child!"

"I was, and that's exactly why she thought she could persuade me. She tried to manipulate me, not knowing what mother had confessed. She said that a marriage to Anne was what my mother wanted and she tried her best to act as a mother to me. But mothers, Georgiana, and fathers –and especially big brothers, should only teach their juniors wrong and right and then let go, and let them decide for themselves. I have maintained and will maintain a relationship with Caroline Bingley for no one's sake now but Bingley. I admit, I thought that she might be a good influence for you, that she might guide you once you were of age, and even trusted her to do so under my watchful eye, taking into consideration what I believe may be a genuine interest in you. But from now on, now that I know she makes you uncomfortable, it will not even be for Bingley's sake that I remain in contact if she makes one wrong step."

"I appreciate it, brother, but there, I think, is no need. Now that I look back on our dealings with her, she is usually sensitive to your opinion. I do not think she will do any irreparable wrong to me. And I hope that her fondness of me is sincere, but I cannot imagine it is. Her aim in getting close to me seems to be little but an attempt to get closer to you, and look affectionate doing so."

It was Darcy's turn to laugh then, surprised at this observation. "You are probably right, Georgie. But have no fear, our cousin Anne and Miss Bingley are absolutely out of the question when it comes to my marrying them. Now," he said, returning to the original subject at hand, "about going to Pemberley."

She waited with bated breath to hear what he had to say.

"You, Georgiana, are grown and may do whatever you wish. I admit that it is much harder to recognize that than it is to say it but you are grown, and marvelously so. The Bennets are your guests, Pemberley is your home, and if you wish to invite the Gardiners and Bingley's to it —that is for you to say. If you wish to order a coach to visit the lakes, that will also be your doing."

"William!" Georgiana jumped up and hugged him, hardly believing her ears. It was too wonderful to be true, to have a brother so kind, attentive, protective and, now, understanding. "But won't you join us, brother?"

"I will, if you wish it and my business allows it."

"I would like nothing better, William. Especially if you leave all the planning to me. Then you could really feel like it was a vacation. You deserve it!"

The bittersweet feeling that had overwhelmed him a moment ago dissipated with her excitement. He had done the right thing —something he should have done long before, he realized.

"I shall write to Bingley to explain that you will be leading a party back home next month and that you plan an excursion to the lakes. But perhaps you should have Elizabeth write to the Gardiners to tell them first. Hopefully they were not thinking of it as a romantic getaway."

"Actually, I do not think they'll mind at all. I know that their initial plan was to take Jane with them but now that we'll all be following in a separate coach, I think they'll be allowed their time alone as well as quality time with their nieces."

"Perfect, then I shall inform Bingley."

"May I invite the Gardiners to stay at Pemberley?" she asked innocently, perfectly aware of the social limitations designating this as improper.

Darcy sighed, wishing, for once, to have a moment alone with Richard or even Miss Bennet (Miss *Elizabeth*, he reminded himself) to debate the matter before he answered. But he could not always have counsel, and neither could his sister.

"You, Miss Georgiana Catherine Darcy, may do whatever you feel is right. You'll notice that I did not say 'as you wish,' for what you desire and what is proper are not always the same thing. I enjoyed the Gardiner's company as much as you did and would seek their company again – absolutely. I have said that you are old enough to make your own decisions and you can hold me to that, but I will always be around to advise you and my advice on this subject would be to think it over. Many more women of the *ton* are like Miss Bingley than are like you or the Bennets. They may not be forgiving to the lapse of propriety. But, like I said before, if you do not respect persons that would make such an uproar...then you may choose not to conform to their expectations."

"Thank you, William. I shall think on it, as you said. But I think, brother, that I have learned that I want to be the type of person (that I am naturally the type of person) to do right based on the standards that I have been taught and apply those to the world as I come to know it rather than have the world apply their sense of wrong or right to me. Elizabeth is the most charming person I have ever met and it makes me sick to think of what the *ton* (or even Miss Bingley) would say about her. I recognize that the wrong lies with them. I will not, from now on, allow others to suppress me into their standard when I've seen that the alternative is so beautiful. I have always heard of those high ranking that kept company with those considered 'out of society' referred to as eccentric and, as long as they are not present, are referred as such in hushed tones as though they were an outcast. But as soon as this person is amongst society —it is though they have done nothing wrong and those who had been so cruel before wear the widest smiling of masks."

"You are absolutely right, Georgiana."

"But members of the *ton* always wear this sort of mask, don't they?"

"Yes. That is at least my observation."

"Then if my actions do not make a difference, I will do what I wish as long as it coincides with what I feel is right – and I will get the same welcoming from the *ton* as long as my wealth proceeds me!" She laughed and Darcy joined her.

I have so much to learn from this little person, he thought. *And many of my own actions to question.* She expressed so well what he had been afraid to embrace —an indifference towards society. The *ton* could not take away anything that mattered to either of them. He had been afraid, he owned, to write off society altogether before Georgiana was of age as he had been afraid it would ruin her chances at a good match. But he no longer concerned himself so much in that regard. Georgiana was not the type to sit around and wait for him to make her a match. She would be a fearsome lady to court, he realized with great relief, and he no longer worried about her being taken advantage of. *No,* he realized, *there is little I can do for her now. Now I must only sit back and watch her life unfold before me.* And for once, he was excited by the complete loss of control.

"Ladies, I have an exciting prospect to offer to you all that I dearly hope you accept," Georgiana announced to the sitting room of Bennet ladies. "I know that you have all been away from home for a long time but I hope you will extend it on my behalf."

"I cannot handle the suspense, Anna!" cried Lydia in an overly dramatic way that she knew would bring Georgiana to hysterics. Jane was the last to join in the laughter, still getting used to the ease of her new company. She was always the more reserved of the Bennet sisters. Even Mary, who would not laugh for anything, was more outspoken, though in a more austere way. Jane smiled often but her shyness had always overruled laughter. She had, since she had always been referred to as a great beauty, come to terms with being looked at –*seen*, but she had not before resolved herself to being *heard*. That was a different matter entirely.

"Lydia, if you insist on making me laugh, you risk ever hearing the news!"

"Do indulge us, Anna, I shall be endeavor to bite my tongue."

"Very well. You are all cordially invited to join me at Pemberley after we have had our fill of balls, banquets, suppers, and theatre shows offered in London. I wager it'll roughly take us less than a month to get through them all which would put our carriage next to the Gardiners', meaning that they would visit with us and we would join them at the lakes, if they did not mind it. Also, I have neglected to mention, my brother's friend and sister will be nearby and will be staying at Pemberley and so will likely join us. That makes it a party of: three Bennet sisters, myself, brother, and cousin, Mr. and Miss Bingley, and the Gardiners. Quite possibly the happiest party to ever disrupt the tranquility of the Lake District. What do you say?"

"I say absolutely!" cried Lydia, wringing her hands and looking to her elder sisters. "I cannot suppress my excitement! That's...ten people!"

"It sounds wonderful," piped up Jane, who was never afraid of delivering a compliment.

"Of course we would love to join you, Georgiana. You are right, however, our parents must be consulted, but I do not foresee their having a problem with it," clarified Elizabeth. As excited as she was, she could not help feeling an overwhelming sense of sadness for their sister, Kitty, who would not doubt be extremely jealous of their travels.

"Kitty will be furious," Lydia said, as though reading her mind.

"You cannot be angry at others for enjoying themselves, Lydia," said Jane.

"She will be granted many opportunities that are lost upon us," Elizabeth said, knowing that it was partially true.

"I had not thought of that," said Georgiana, "I would never want to cause a rift."

"Do not concern yourself with our sisters," assured Elizabeth, "we will gladly accept your invitation with no qualms. Kitty is not as mature as we'd like her to be at her age. She needs every opportunity to grow older." She meant what she said, but she could still not help feeling bad. It would be an opportunity for Kitty to learn, but she would probably not see it that way. Elizabeth decided that she would write to her father and stress that he take advantage of the time he had alone with his younger daughters. Between Lydia and Kitty, Lydia was certainly the less controllable but since she had grown so well in the past few weeks, Elizabeth had hope for Kitty also. When they returned, if Kitty was not improved, the new behavior of her younger sister as well as the heavy-handed influence of the oldest ones would no doubt aid her. She did not yet know what would be done for Mary, but thought that Lydia's newfound conduct might influence her for the better. "I will write to our father and the Gardiners presently. Lydia and Jane, our mother would no doubt appreciate hearing from you."

The Gardiners responded in good time to Elizabeth's announcement and graciously accepted to invitation to Pemberley as well as the company to the lakes. Along with their letter, they sent a large basket of fruit, tea, and bourbon as a thank you, the most delectable of the exports that Mr. Gardiner handled.

"I did not think it was possible to like them more!" Richard exclaimed upon seeing the bottle of specialty bourbon. "You Bennets are a magical sort of company, aren't you?"

"I will write to them immediately, Miss Elizabeth," Darcy said, "if you would kindly provide me with their address. This is too kind." Darcy had never been more touched in all of his life. Never once had he been given a gift for such a simple reason. The Gardiners, he thought, were the best sort of people he had ever met, and he was sure that their nieces were well on their way to growing up to be just like them.

He and Colonel Fitzwilliam disappeared to his study with the bourbon and the address while the ladies decided what was to be done with the fruit, choosing to turn it into either jam, pie, or to let it be enjoyed fresh.

"Isn't life wonderful?" Richard asked Darcy as he poured them each a glass.

"It is, Fitzwilliam."

"I am so happy to see you so happy, cousin. I knew that you were in there somewhere, somewhere inside that thick head of yours. These Gardiners are amazing people. I cannot even begin speaking of their nieces. Why, if I were a younger man, I'd fancy myself in love with every one of them."

Darcy rolled his eyes before responding, having heard enough of the topic of "love" for the season. "Since when did you grow up?"

"To see them with my niece, Darcy, I have been scared into thinking of myself as being my actual age. Laughing alongside Georgiana —they are too young."

"What if she is just older, cousin?"

"That thought crossed my mind. And then I wouldn't allow it to again. Speak no more of our Georgiana growing."

"I believe you were the first to bring it up, Fitzwilliam, when last we had a serious discussion about the way I was treating her."

"That was the first and last it crossed my mind, Darcy. Don't you ever pay attention to me? Are the Bennet ladies not the most wonderful women you have ever met?"

"I suppose they are, yes." Darcy felt as though a great weight was lifted off his shoulders when he admitted it. He had fought this thought for so long –unnecessarily. What harm could it do anyone to admit that someone was good? In truth, he did not wish to admit that someone whom he had never heard of before could be the most quality person. It was as though they would detract from the worth of those he had. But this was silly –the Bennets were the kindest, most charming women of his acquaintance, taking into account all the wealthy, titled, and related persons he knew.

"And the most beautiful, I think. Especially as they are not even trying! Why –the ladies of the *ton* get so gussied up I can hardly see their faces and they often dress as though they intend to blind you. Jane is the most beautiful creature I have ever set eyes on and the sweetest personality to match, Elizabeth is the most captivating of any person I have ever met, her eyes and laugh are enough to arrest me, and Lydia, is the most lively, whimsical little sprite. And our little Georgiana, she is the most impressive of all –full of class, kindness, modesty, an attractiveness all her own. We are lucky men, Darcy, to be amongst such excellent company; to even know that these types of women exist. Seeing them all this morning, I cannot not think of myself marrying any girl that could not hold her own amongst them. They have ruined my idea of my perfect match. How can I settle for the richest woman who will have me when, no matter how thick her pocket book, she will come up short in comparison? We are blessed with the knowledge that there are women like them out there, if only we have the patience and foresight to find them."

The sweet aftertaste of the bourbon faded away long before the effect of Colonel Fitzwilliam's speech and William Darcy entered the sitting room not only with the intention to join the ladies but, specifically, to get to know one of them better.

Chapter 19

"I'm sorry, I did not know anyone else was up," Elizabeth bowed and moved to leave the library, coming upon Mr. Darcy reading in the firelight. It was late, but somehow sleep had evaded her. Darcy stood up half in a stupor, revealing that he had removed his coat and top two buttons.

"Miss Elizabeth, please. Do not leave on my account."

It would not have been uncomfortable to stay, she thought, but was embarrassed for him that he had obviously forgotten about his buttons. She could only stare at the brown wisps of chest hair protruding from the billowing shirt and not even move towards the shelves. He looked down after a moment, embarrassed and blushing, only to have her do the same. She was at the shelves in a moment then, with her back to him, face afire with mortification, while he buttoned up, making some incoherent excuse for his appearance and apologizing profusely.

"This is your home, Mr. Darcy," was all she could manage to say in response, looking too hard at a book she didn't intend to pick out. She could hear him rustling with the logs and adding more to the fire; to stay busy, she reasoned.

After more than enough firewood was added, he spoke: "Late to bed, early to rise? It is a rare characteristic."

"I would not say rare."

He laughed and took the bait, not knowing what she would say next but knowing that it would be humorous and cheeky. "Oh?"

"There are six individuals here, two of whom share that quality. I'd say those are good odds."

"Allow me to rephrase. It is a good characteristic."

"A self-serving proclamation to which I will self-servingly agree." She looked at the fire, finding a roaring hot blaze. "Do you intend to sleep at all tonight, Mr. Darcy?" He looked significantly taken aback as though he did not understand why she would ask such a thing —as though he was thinking that she had specifically meant something else, but she could not think of what that could be.

"Sorry?" Indeed something else was on his mind, but not intentionally. It was not every night that the object of one's affections surprised you late and alone in your cozy library. He had just been thinking about Miss Elizabeth Bennet right before she appeared, as though he had willed her there. It was not until he had caught her looking at his chest that his thoughts had turned instantly from innocent to questionable. He had just been thinking, he recalled, about how he could not determine whether or not he truly liked her and then *boom* – there she was, staring at him, nervous. *What's not to like about her?* He asked himself and could not answer.

"You've loaded the hearth with enough fuel for winter, Mr. Darcy. How long do you plan on holding up in here?"

"Oh." This seemed the least appropriate, least logical explanation for what she had said. He was nearly disappointed. He had been hoping for (without reason, he now owned), some sign that his affections (if he had them, that is) were returned. "I got carried away. I had intended to make sure you weren't cold, but I guess now that goes for here or your bedroom for I seem to have ensured that the entire house stays warm."

"That is very kind of you, Mr. Darcy. But do not concern yourself, I shall not stay long as I could not disturb you."

"You would not disturb me, Miss Bennet —Elizabeth," he caught himself. "I would appreciate company, if you do not object to it."

She soon found out that, in this instance, company meant someone to talk to —not someone to read next to. She had barely cracked open her book, reclined against the plush sofa, and read the first word: "The..." before Darcy spoke.

"Is your elder sister comfortable, Miss Elizabeth?" he asked, thinking that would be the most appropriate, most relevant subject to begin conversation. He had not read one page since he had closed himself in the library, being completely distracted by thoughts of the woman who now sat across from him and what he might like to know about her.

"She is, thank you," Elizabeth said, recognizing that Darcy was acting strange, then added, "You have probably noticed that she is shy in comparison to Lydia and myself, so those who don't know her well sometimes have a hard time gauging her feelings." She had a funny feeling that she had just described both her beloved sister as well as the gentleman before her.

"I understand," he said, though the thought needed more reflection. The eldest Bennet smiled so much, he would have guessed that she was always pleased. "She has an easy smile, Miss Elizabeth, I would have thought that that was a reflection of her mood."

Elizabeth began to suspect that either Mr. Darcy was becoming a studier of character (her favorite pastime) or that he had become infatuated with her elder sister. Jane was known at home as the most beautiful woman in Meryton and she had, though she was still considered young, her fair share of suitors. It was no loss, Elizabeth had thought, that they hadn't stuck around, for she saw no redeeming quality in any of them. Many had left, in her opinion, due to the subject at hand: it was difficult to guess Jane's feelings, and no man could stand unrequited affection for long without doing damage to his ego. Their feelings were not long lasting, in Elizabeth's opinion, if they could not stand to be patient and, ultimately, could not have deserved her.

"It takes time to know her, Mr. Darcy. And though her constant smile is just one of her many engaging attributes, it is not always a reflection of her feelings. Above all else, Jane is always polite. She is stronger in that sense, than any I know."

"I don't think you give yourself enough credit, Miss Elizabeth. You are the most attentive, patient, sociable person I have ever before met. Perhaps you, too, require getting to know before understanding your various looks and tones, but to the untrained eye, you appear kind to all you come across, patient in the face of any difficulty, and no less than charming where it is both possible and not."

Elizabeth set her book down to look at him and found his gaze earnest, fervent. Something had changed in him, but she could not understand what. This was not the same man that had attempted to shovel her and Lydia out the door just as he had Wickham. This was the man she had expected to meet when she had first heard of Miss Darcy having a brother, but she feared that it was, like his sour mood, another temporary state. But she had prided herself on being an adamant studier of character and so decided that he would just be another interesting study. If he had changed for the better and for good after treating her so poorly, it was all the more positive as well as interesting. She did not know if she liked him –his company was certainly less predictable than Colonel Fitzwilliam's and he was a great deal more complicated, but she could at least rule out, for the moment, not liking him.

"Then I thank God that you cannot read my mind," Elizabeth said, half-teasing. He chuckled and shook his head.

"You are remarkable, Miss Elizabeth, for never ceasing to surprise me. I had grown quite jaded and believed nothing else ever could."

"Jaded at the ripe old age of nine and twenty?"

"You are partially to blame."

"Oh?"

"Because I had never before met anyone like you." He let this compliment set, but was somewhat displeased with it – perhaps because it was not immediately returned. *The lady did not even have the decency to blush,* he fumed, before chiding himself. *It makes no difference to me whether or not she should blush. In any case, she is no woman of the ton; she does not have to blush to be noticed. Or,* fear crept into his thoughts, *I have not given her reason to and she is not at all easily impressed.* He could see this was a definite possibility. "Georgiana is lucky," he added, taking the emphasis off of his targeted flattery, "she only had to wait sixteen years."

"You, in turn, are surprising, Mr. Darcy," she said in the absence of expressing gratitude she did not feel was necessary. He was too peculiar, she thought, to have specifically meant anything to be a compliment. He was beginning to remind her of her friend and neighbor, Charlotte Lucas' father, who was known to the neighborhood in general to be a great grouch. It was not until Charlotte and Elizabeth got close that she saw a different side of him: rough though his edges may have been, Sir Lucas was soft when it came to his daughter. He would often call Elizabeth and Charlotte into his study to "interview" them (as he called it) about their day —what they had learned, what they should endeavor to learn tomorrow. He had a strange sense of humor lost upon them most of the time and was difficult to get to know, but was good hearted overall, in a secretive sort of way. Relating Darcy to Sir Lucas was the easiest way that Elizabeth could justify his behavior. Perhaps this is the type of treatment she could expect to receive as his sister's friend. He was brash, upon first meeting, closed off and irreproachable, but was adamant about meeting people on his own terms. "*Eccentric*" —she decided. Now that his terms were met, he could approach her with some form of kindness, abrupt though it may be.

"I hope in a good way," he said. He thought about what she had said before about reading her mind and was suddenly frightened by the prospect. He had been rather incorrigible, according to his sister and cousin, and could not imagine what her quick mind and sharp eyes had perceived.

Elizabeth wasn't ready to have this conversation with him and doubted she would ever be prepared at all. She and Mr. Darcy did not need to be friends; it was only necessary that they have a mutual respect for one another. Elizabeth could look on at Mr. Darcy and admire him for being a good brother to Georgiana and he could admire Elizabeth for being a good friend to his sister. They need not go beyond that –and they wouldn't. It did not matter whether or not she *liked* the man or whether he liked her. It was arm's length, removed esteem that was necessary.

"Thus far," she answered. "Thank you for playing host to my sisters and I for so long, Mr. Darcy, and for opening your home to us and my beloved Aunt and Uncle."

"Of course, Miss Elizabeth, but your thanks can be directed towards my sister. It is all her doing."

"You are no doubt partially to blame. I am grateful that there are such good people in the world, Mr. Darcy. It is exactly what Lydia needs to see."

"The same goes for Georgiana. I had not expected her transformation to be so easily made. You would not have recognized her a year ago, Miss Elizabeth. She was beyond shy –petrified. And I partially blame myself for this. I closed her off to the world, only gave her access to family which proved to be detrimental; my family can be a frightening bunch." He laughed, thinking of Lady Catherine and Lady Fitzwilliam. They were upstanding women in society, to be sure, but were rather unapproachable, one more so than the other. If he could have only remembered how fearful of them he had been at a young age, he would have never pushed Georgiana to spend so much time with them. They could be very critical and, at times, very brash.

"I sympathize, Mr. Darcy. My family is not virtuous, by any means. But I am glad that you like those you have met so far. As I grow older, I begin to recognize that family can be the circle of friends you surround yourself with."

Darcy was speechless – never had he before met someone so philosophical. Even if one did not agree with Miss Elizabeth, she could persuade you into seeing something from a different perspective. An argument with her wasn't a dispute, it was a discussion. Richard had been right about her. Darcy wished that he had seen it before and, beyond that, that he had known her for longer; that he could have had her company at every turn. He would have appreciated her point of view, could have used her wisdom. He could not have put his opinion of her into words, but could only sense that a relationship with her was important. This Miss Bennet was significant to him, and he felt as though she would only grow in significance, though he was unsure of how. All he knew, at this moment, was that he needed to enjoy every moment with her and to endeavor to secure more.

They discussed half the night away, their books cast aside: everything from growing up in the country to coming out into society. Their lives could not be more different, they decided, but there was some kindred connection between them that was undeniable. They may hardly see eye-to-eye on any topic, but where they did disagree, it was amiable and full of understanding; it was an appreciation that neither had known before.

The fire was nearly out before either of them recognized the lapse in time that Elizabeth was the first to point out.

"Mr. Darcy, in a matter of minutes, I could ask you to join me on my morning walk."

"And I would happily consent," Darcy said, laughing. "I would apologize for keeping you so long, Miss Elizabeth, but I have enjoyed our time too much for it to have been sincere."

"And I would never have accepted it, for I, too, have enjoyed our time. I will see you on the morrow, Mr. Darcy."

As Elizabeth made her way to bed, she considered that evening one of the most pleasant of her life and, though she wouldn't exactly have sought out Mr. Darcy's company, she would not have minded spending another evening in that capacity.

Chapter 20

"You two!" Colonel Fitzwilliam shouted when Elizabeth and Darcy happened to enter the breakfast room nearly an hour after what was their usual custom. "I knew you were human."

"I did not know you expected differently, Colonel," said Elizabeth in greeting. The rest of the household was up; halfway through their breakfast by the time Darcy and Elizabeth sat down with full plates.

In fashionable homes, breakfast was supposed to be the more silent meal of the day, but there was an exception in the Darcy household for as long as a Bennet was under their roof. The Bennets were not fully to blame, however, even a strict socialite would have acknowledged that it was usually Colonel Fitzwilliam that provoked conversation, as though he had waited all night for it, missing his companions dearly.

"It is only that I have so rarely seen the two of you sleep in," Fitzwilliam explained. "Tell me you did lose another chess match, Darce."

"I'm sorry to disappoint you so early in the morning, cousin. No –I did not lose another chess match."

"I am still pleased to see you, in any case, Darcy," Fitzwilliam said, "Georgiana and I were just explaining to Miss Bennet and Miss Lydia what to expect at the supper party tonight."

"I look forward to tonight, Colonel," Elizabeth said kindly, "I have heard much of your mother's dinner parties and look forward to meeting her as well."

"Then you must have heard all about her parties and nothing about her, Miss Elizabeth," he said in jest. Darcy and

Georgiana interrupted then, attempting to defend their aunt with phrases such as, "comes off strong," and "is difficult to get to know" which only added to Fitzwilliam's laughter. "She will adore you, Miss Bennet, for your beauty and your charm, do not concern yourself. Miss Lydia, your youthful energy will suppress her criticisms and…Miss Elizabeth, your wit will scare her into silence! I might let you lead the party in."

"Am I so terrible as that?" Elizabeth asked, giggling at the portrait that Colonel Fitzwilliam had painted of her.

"No!" Darcy shouted before he could stop himself. Colonel Fitzwilliam laughed at his outburst while the girls sat in stunned silence, not knowing what to make of it. "I only meant that," Darcy began, "…that if she is silenced by your genius, then it is her loss for not being able to draw more out of you with every next sentence."

Colonel Fitzwilliam and the Bennets fell into conversation while Darcy sat in a dazed relief, not knowing that he was the close study of his younger sister. She had seen the change in him, of course, as everyone else had, but assigned a different reason to it entirely. She hadn't seen him this happy in years, she granted, but neither had she seen him this discomposed. To the untrained eye, it may have seemed that the biggest changes were made after Miss Jane Bennet's arrival, but Georgiana had perceived a change in his behavior long before then.

She doubted he even knew –didn't think the lady even suspected, that William Darcy was half in love with Elizabeth Bennet.

The way he looked at her: a mixture of confusion and comfort; as though he was desperately searching to put a name to something he could feel was there. But mere feelings had never been good enough for Mr. Darcy. He needed fact, proof.

She looked at Elizabeth, full of wonder, hope, and laughter, and wondered if she could ever love her brother. She would be good for him, surely, but Elizabeth was so self-assured and independent that Georgiana didn't know if *he* would be good for her. Elizabeth was like the heroines that were Georgiana's favorite to read about: beautiful, fierce, strong, and determined. In fiction, these women had always succumbed (in a way) to true love and usually maintained their independence after doing so, or at least, it was alluded to. Georgiana wondered if, in this case, art mimicked life. *Could Elizabeth possibly be persuaded into matrimony?* She had said before it would only be by the deepest love –but was she too headstrong to recognize it if it came to pass? Georgiana began to fear for her brother then. She knew that he remained unaware of his own feelings, but worried for him when they surfaced. He could marry where he wanted, surely, but she knew that Elizabeth was not whom he had imagined for himself. Of the two, it was impossible to tell who was more headstrong. Likely, he would forsake her for his reputation. She shuddered at the thought.

"Is everything alright, Georgiana?" Richard asked her across the sitting room. She jumped –realizing that she had been lost deep in thought nearly all day. All eyes turned to her, waiting for an answer.

"I was daydreaming, I am afraid. Hopefully I will be more sociable at supper."

For the remainder of the afternoon prior to excusing themselves to prepare for Lady Fitzwilliam's supper, Georgiana watched Darcy and Elizabeth interact carefully. There was much between them that neither yet acknowledged, certainly, but Georgiana was determined that when it was realized, it was not immediately discarded. There was no danger for either party now –but that could not be said for long.

"I admit, Lizzy, I was nervous to join the party," Jane nearly whispered to Elizabeth as she saw to her hair. "But now that I am fully welcomed, I feel it was completely unnecessary.

Why –where have people like these been hiding for all of our lives?"

Jane, who had never spoken ill of anybody, had just uttered her least-kind observation. It was primarily a compliment, to be sure, but hidden beneath was the suggestion that no one else they knew was worth as much as their present companions. Elizabeth could not disagree –it would be very difficult to return to Longbourn having been spoiled by all this good company.

"I am hardly nervous for tonight," she continued. "Worst case scenario, we are left to ourselves or huddled with our companions. I say it'll be more entertaining than any evening we've spent at the Lucas'."

"I agree with you, wholeheartedly," Elizabeth said, switching places with her sister once Jane's curls were set.

It was the first time they had been left alone for the better part of an hour as Georgiana and Lydia had opted to have their hair done by the maids.

"Would it be selfish if I wished that we met more people like them tonight?" teased Elizabeth.

"Not at all, if we are half so charming. You are very delightful company, Elizabeth. You have helped Lydia immensely, I cannot believe how much she is changed."

"It is mostly owning to her friendship with Georgiana," Elizabeth explained. "It has also been tremendous to have had such close conduct with Mr. Darcy and Colonel Fitzwilliam. She has begun to realize that men are not all targets that we must throw ourselves up against, as Mama has so expertly put in our heads."

Jane covered her mouth and giggled, the gesture being one of the few remaining habits that had been drilled into her head by their mother. She had changed as well. Not nearly as much as Lydia, as she did not need to come as far, but enough for Elizabeth to feel it was a good thing. Elizabeth wondered if she had changed as well.

"They are the kindest men of my acquaintance and the most entertaining," said Jane. "When I first saw them with you, though, I believed them to be doing nothing by vying for your affections. They are so doting, aren't they? But now that I have gotten to know them better –well, it is only brotherly affection, is it not?"

"I believe it is friendly affection as directed towards their sister and cousin's companions. We are altogether too familiar with each other, to be measured by society's standards. I just hope that tonight we are not prone to keeping our little party separate from the rest. I am truly interested in making new acquaintances now that I am content with the ones I have. Counterintuitive, I know, but I have a backup plan now, you see."

Jane laughed again, this time, forgetting to cover her mouth. She was beautiful when she laughed and there was a sophisticated ring to the sound. Elizabeth had always thought her sister as better belonging to the upper classes and any that met her were soon convinced of the same.

Even Elizabeth blushed when they were announced to the crowd of formally dressed onlookers, each peering over the next to get a look at them.

"I often appear unaccompanied or solely with my cousin, Miss Elizabeth," Darcy whispered, as though sensing her wonder. He often did this, she realized, provided an answer to a question that she had but did not voice. Their thoughts must often be similar, she reasoned.

Next to her, Darcy chastised himself for drawing so closely to her. He all but shook as he felt the eyes on him, his aunt had seen to inviting an extra number of single women to dine this evening. It was for his cousin's benefit, he realized, as Lady Fitzwilliam openly admitted that she cared for nothing more than to see her second son retire his red coat and marry, but few eyes would settle on the second son of an earl whilst

Darcy was present. His fortune was his own; his parents were deceased, making him more than eligible by the *ton's* standards. Fitzwilliam often joked with his mother that, until Darcy married, no women would look his way, and so instructed her to find Darcy a match if she really wished to see him settled down.

"What they don't understand," Darcy had said to his cousin after a particularly frightening night of dodging single women and their even more tactless mothers at a ball, "is that I have no interest in anyone only interested in me for their money."

"Come again?" Fitzwilliam had said, swigging back brandy.

"I understand why that makes me a target but I don't understand why they set aside tact, reason, and manners. At least pretend that my worth extends beyond my pocket book and you might score a dance with me."

If it weren't for his sister and her friends at his side, he would have gladly made an excuse to leave this evening, run away to the shelter of his library. He had not prepared himself for a night of vigilant onlookers or false niceties. Any attention he now paid to the women he was with would cost them all dearly. They would be scrutinized, questioned, and denounced all in a matter of minutes.

Elizabeth had surely noticed the piercing looks she had received after Darcy had taken the liberty of whispering in her ear. She had never before been the object of such study. She always received a secondary sort of attention, being usually at Jane's side. It had been that way when they had walked in, but no longer. She could hear the whispers, "Who's that with Mr. Darcy?" and she wished to point out the absurdity of such a question. If they wished to know, why not just speak to the woman in question?

Colonel Fitzwilliam led them through to a sitting room that was generally acknowledged as a section for relatives.

They were introduced to Sir and Lady Fitzwilliam and the Colonel's older brother, Eric, who had similar features to his brother but lacked the same warmth. Georgiana, Elizabeth was pleased to see, stiffened during the conversation with her aunt but did not completely slip back into her old, timid self.

Sir Fitzwilliam asked a number of pertinent and polite questions of the Bennet girls, zeroing in on Jane easily as she was the eldest and most beautiful. Shy though she was, Jane was never one to show it in matters of propriety. Those that knew her well could detect whether or not she was uncomfortable, but Sir Fitzwilliam would have never known the difference. Their party was disturbed when Lady Catherine and Anne de Bourgh were announced and the Bennet girls noticed bizarre expressions cross the faces of their hosts. Georgiana and Darcy exchanged looks whilst Colonel Fitzwilliam uttered, "damn" under his breath.

From the initial look of her, Lady Catherine's gait caused no alarm. It was her eyes, Elizabeth finally realized, that were unsettling. Her daughter, they presumed to be Anne, was nothing but a slip of a shadow that scurried in her wake. The room's occupants seemed to subconsciously clear space for them and, by the time they could process it, the great women (in both stature and standing) was before them.

"Darcy, how surprised I am to see you, all it took was a four hour carriage ride for a chance to speak with my nephew this year. Sir and Lady Fitzwilliam, charmed." Her greetings were spoken quickly, clearly, and without feeling, as though a sergeant delivering orders. "Georgiana, you are quite grown since last I saw you. Fitting since you are out when I may not have advised it. Who have we here?" She settled her gaze on the Bennet sisters one at a time and Georgiana stepped in before her brother could speak, eager that she not let her newfound courage fail her now.

"Aunt Catherine, these are my friends. May I introduce to you, Miss Bennet, Miss Elizabeth, and Miss Lydia. My aunt,

Lady Catherine de Bourgh and her daughter, Anne." The diminutive figure that was Anne popped out from behind her mother to crane her neck downwards in an elegant bow of the head and, just after settling a nearly imperceptive gaze at Darcy and Richard, disappeared behind her mother before any onlookers could really register that she had ever been visible.

"I did not know it was your habit to keep female company, Darcy," Lady Catherine cut.

"They are my guests, Lady Catherine," Georgiana insisted. Her voice was higher, weaker, and more timid, but there was no mistaking her attempt to match the woman's tone. "I was fortunate enough to have met Miss Elizabeth in town and she has been my companion nearly the entirety of summer. We are joined by her sisters more recently and will retire to Pemberley together once our business is finished in town."

"And your brother and cousin will no doubt be joining you, I daresay," Lady Catherine said, laughing, though it was not in jest. "Anne and I have been awaiting your visit, gentleman. But you know I was never one to exercise patience."

Elizabeth saw the same anger cross Darcy's face as she had observed when she had first seen him on the seaside when Georgiana was explaining the situation with Wickham. This was a difficult matter for them all to bear, she realized, and justifiably so. Lady Catherine was such a blunt force of nature that it was clear no one wanted anything to do with her. Even her daughter, out of sight, seemed cowered every time the lady opened her mouth. While Darcy explained that he and Fitzwilliam intended to visit at Easter as they had every year, Georgiana and the Fitzwilliams worked to maneuver the Bennet girls out of range.

Taking them aside, Lady Fitzwilliam whispered, "Girls, the key to a successful supper party is surprises. Lady Catherine will no doubt give people something to talk about.

Georgie," she said to her niece, "if you can, try and speak to Anne when she is not overshadowed by her mother. That poor thing wilts away worse than my roses. Girls, I do hope you enjoy yourselves despite the summer storm that has just rolled in." *There's the relation to Colonel Fitzwilliam* —was the general thought of the Bennet sisters as they were led through the party and into the dining hall where they located their assigned seating to find servants bustling about, hurriedly moving name cards to accommodate the uninvited and newly arrived de Bourghs.

While it was more customary to sit next to a stranger, the Bennet girls were relieved to find that they were all designated quite close to one another, only separated by a few ladies and gentlemen that they had not yet been introduced to. Elizabeth was seated closest to Miss Anne and politely declined Georgiana's offer to switch with her, knowing that Georgiana would appreciate being seated where her name card already sat. Lady Catherine and the gentlemen were placed half the table away, most likely guaranteeing them a Lady Catherine-free supper.

They joined the rest of the party, resolving to follow Georgiana's lead until supper was announced. Mingling amongst this crowd reminded Elizabeth of an assembly, for she always found herself paired off and away from her sister's and friend, locked into a conversation with either one gentleman or one lady at a time.

The gentlemen of the gathering, the Bennets found, were polite enough and mostly wished to learn where they were from, whereas the ladies, after a question or two, would hone in on how they were acquainted with the Darcys' and, more specifically, how much time they had spent in Mr. Darcy's company. Jane was the most sought after, after Georgiana, for her beauty and birthright. Gentlemen instinctively knew that she was the first in line to marry and ladies feared her most, for it was most likely that she, of any of the Bennet girls, would marry their intended.

"Cousin!" shouted Eric Fitzwilliam to Georgiana once she had gained a moment's peace from the crowd. He had his brother's volume, Elizabeth found, but none of his sincerity from what she had seen so far. "My brother hogs you, doesn't he? You are grown, milady. You and your friends make up the most beautiful group of ladies here, has anyone told you that yet?"

"Thank you, Eric," Georgiana said as enthusiastically as she could as he bade the Bennet girls to join them. "And so you should leave London so soon, I hear?" he asked after exchanging a few pleasantries between them. They took turns explaining their plans for the remainder of the summer but Elizabeth noticed that, no matter who was speaking, Eric Fitzwilliam's gaze would always fall upon Jane and remain there. After a while, it was just as though he were only speaking to her.

"Eric!" boomed Colonel Fitzwilliam's voice seemingly out of nowhere as his great hand came up to slap his brother's shoulder a bit harder than seemed necessary for a greeting. "Our cousin knows quite what to expect from you, but I cannot allow you to scare off the Bennets. They are all too dear to my heart, each one of them." There was no mistaking what the Colonel actually meant, he may as well have uttered "back off," but, as he was not a jealous man, Elizabeth knew that his purpose must have been for their safety and nothing else.

"I shall endeavor to be on my best behavior then," he quipped, taking Jane's hand and lifting to his lips before departing, "Until next time." With a wink, he was gone.

"There won't be a next time, I'm afraid," Colonel Fitzwilliam muttered more to himself than to the Bennets.

"Your brother puts forth too much effort to come off as charming as you," said Lydia kindly, making him smile.

"You are too kind, Lydia dear." It was too innocent a comment to have faulted him for neglecting propriety. "Girls, protecting you is exhausting. Would you possibly turn down your charm just a tad bit? Your brother, Georgiana, was about to tear my head off just now as he did not think I was quick enough to separate you from my brother."

"He is harmless," said Elizabeth, wishing to put his mind at ease.

"To you, perhaps, but not so far to many."

"I have seen his smiling mask worn too often by that mutual acquaintance we all share," said Lydia, forgetting that Jane was not familiar with the particulars of Mr. Wickham's crimes. Jane was far too polite, however, to have raised concern at not understanding and continued in her usual way, always wanting to think the best of people.

"I trust you, Colonel, but it would be difficult to gauge when someone you know so well has changed. Perhaps he has opted for a more virtuous path since you last saw him."

"My dear, Miss Bennet, I wish the world was really the way you see it. I shall hope and pray for it, but I shall not bet your well being on it. As far as it concerns you and your sisters, my brother is not to be trusted."

Georgiana and the Bennet girls were in for a shock when it came time to dine, for, the place cards that they had not an hour before studied had been moved. Jane was now across the table from them all, seated next to Eric Fitzwilliam and nearer to the other gentlemen of their party. Elizabeth, too, was switched and found herself out of view of both Lydia and Georgiana, and separated from Anne de Bourgh by a man she had not before met and would not meet until halfway through the first course, as he was engrossed in all but verbally attacking the poor, shy Anne. When Miss de Bourgh did not answer one of his three or so questions posed to her, he rattled on as though he had not meant to hear her opinion in any case.

Elizabeth cleared her throat and took the opportunity to rescue Miss Anne from her distress as best she could when the man glanced sideways at her.

"Forgive my intrusion, I could not help but overhear your interest in horseback riding." It was the topic of his statements at least three minutes back, but she had not understood what he at most previously been speaking about and, she guessed, Anne hadn't either.

"It is an interest of yours as well?" He did not look nearly as excited as Anne looked relieved at her interference.

"I'm afraid I am rather of the opinion of Miss de Bourgh," Elizabeth said, throwing a smart glance in the lady's direction so that she might ascertain that she had interrupted them for her benefit. "I prefer walking, if it is a possibility."

The man scoffed and turned as though to cut her out of the conversation again, before Anne intervened.

"I would have said the same, Miss Elizabeth. Though I'm rather fond of short walks and no riding at all. Many women of my acquaintance prefer long rides and short walks."

"It is not that I set out to be different," Elizabeth answered quickly, "but I would have to state my preference as appreciating long walks and short rides."

The man looked between them, utterly lost as to how he could again regain control of the conversation.

"In a downpour," Anne said with a slight smirk, "I am sure most would say that they would like neither."

"In that, we can all agree. I am glad we have found common ground." Elizabeth smiled at her and had it returned unabashedly, though the man's pathetic mutterings obscured the sentiment somewhat.

"And you are?" he demanded haughtily of Elizabeth.

"Forgive me, Sir Hathrope," said Anne, "this is Miss Elizabeth Bennet. She and her sisters are guests of the Darcy's."

The man's eyes widened significantly and flew to observe Mr. Darcy and crane his neck to catch sight of Miss Darcy before landing back on Elizabeth to let her know what a pleasure it was to make her acquaintance. He sat in affected silence whilst Anne and Elizabeth discussed how Elizabeth had come to be acquainted with her family.

"I did not know them to entertain often, but I see that you and your sisters are of a special caliber of company, Miss Elizabeth."

Anne was all that her mother ought to be when she was safe from her mother's shadow, Elizabeth thought. If it weren't for her, Elizabeth was sure they could become friends.

Sir Hathrope, it was apparent, did not know to which lady he should pay more compliments to, and so the same were delivered to each, separately. If he complimented Anne's dress, he would turn to make notice of Elizabeth's earrings, and so on. Though Elizabeth could see nothing of her sister or Georgiana, she heard her sister's laughter often followed by Georgiana's polite titters and trusted that they were enjoying themselves.

Jane, who could always be trusted to do well in public, was perhaps having the most difficult time as she faced what Elizabeth perceived was constant reprimanding by Lady Catherine. As far as Elizabeth could tell, the lady was determined to see that an unknown woman would have any attention from any nephew of hers and so was seeking to humiliate Jane so as to eliminate the prospect of a match. Jane was the perfect one for that albeit difficult position, Elizabeth realized, as she herself could have easily taken too much offense at what the lady said to her. It would not do to offend the host's own family members, though, by the expressions on the faces of the Fitzwilliams, Elizabeth doubted they would have minded.

Anne followed Elizabeth's gaze and shook her head ever so slightly when she caught sight of her mother.

"My mother…" she began.

"Looks younger every time I see her," Sir Hathrope inserted. It was all Elizabeth and Anne could do not to laugh at this. "You two could be sisters."

"As much as some may say you look alike," Elizabeth said, stifling giggles, "I find that you are very different in personality."

Anne nodded a silent understanding and allowed Sir Hathrope to pick up where he had last left off, recounting an evening either he or his father had spent in the de Bourghs' home.

Jane did not complain of a splitting headache as some ladies were so often known to do, but it was tempting. Between faking smiles in the direction of Eric Fitzwilliam and directing real ones between Darcy, the Colonel, and his parents, she was beginning to find it difficult to divert time to chewing her food. When Lady Catherine started in on her, she lost the ability to eat altogether.

"Your youngest sisters are out before the eldest are married? Why, that is very unorthodox," Lady Catherine said of Lydia's presence before Jane had even broached the subject of having younger sisters. "How many of you are there?"

"I have four younger sisters, Lady Catherine," she answered, preferring Eric Fitzwilliam's abrasive stare to this woman's attacks, even if it did accompany Mr. Darcy and Colonel Fitzwilliam's sour looks.

"No sons?"

"No, ma'am."

"It is very unfashionable for the lower classes to have no male heirs," she said, continuing on in an offensive manner that Jane half-wished Elizabeth could witness as she was sure that she would have something intelligent to say to put a stop to it.

"With daughters so lovely," Colonel Fitzwilliam said, coming to Jane's defense, "the Bennet family is the most fortunate I have ever met with."

"The only disservice that is done by all the Bennet's being out at once is that their beauty is quite overwhelming," added Eric Fitzwilliam, determined to outdo his brother. Sir and Lady Fitzwilliam, lost in conversation with Darcy, had nothing to contribute to their sons' battle of wits. Lady Catherine could only suppress an eye roll before continuing:

"Your governess must have been busy," she said, to have taught you." She did not pause long enough for Jane to admit that they had not grown up with a governess. "Anne's governess was quite thorough, though music was not included, as it was not with me. She does not have the proper disposition for it. If she would have learned, she would have been a great proficient."

"I have always found it more pleasant to listen," Jane said politely.

There was not much Lady Catherine could fault Jane for so returned to the topic of the Bennet family being rather unsuitable or, to use her word, unconventional. Jane was relieved when the main course was served for it spared her the focus of Lady Catherine's attentions and, instead, found herself bombarded with Eric Fitzwilliam's undivided attention.

"I am an appetizer, dessert sort of man, Miss Bennet. I go easy during the main meal to save room. I'm a sucker for something sweet, you know?"

"Then you have must have never sampled this, Mr. Fitzwilliam, or you would never resist it." Jane spoke about the duck, but it became clear all too quickly that he took her to be referring to something else. She blushed uncomfortably, suddenly wishing that duck was not Lady Catherine's favorite morsel. She would have preferred that lady's criticisms right about then. Eric Fitzwilliam was not the gentleman that she had hoped he was and, like his brother feared, he had apparently not changed.

Darcy, perceiving the quiet had meant something of the sort had happened, broke off the conversation with his aunt and uncle to engage the suddenly silenced Miss Bennet.

"Miss Bennet, duck, I know, is a favorite of your sisters. Is it one of yours as well?"

She was grateful beyond words –he could tell just from her expression. So grateful, that she nearly forgot to answer the question.

"It is of my sisters," she began after a moment, "and before tonight I may have not agreed with them, but after the way I have enjoyed how this was prepared, well…it is one of my favorites now." It was the most honest thing she had ever said, she decided. After Lady Catherine's uncalled-for reprimanding and Eric Fitzwilliam's heavy-handed notice, she had cast aside falsities and decided to be courteous but honest. It was what Elizabeth had always suggested that she do, and she found it invigorating to speak her mind in a gracious manner.

"My brother tells me you are to visit the lakes soon, Miss Bennet," said Eric, addressing Jane once again.

"We are. Miss Darcy has been kind enough to arrange it."

"I am tempted to go along as well, it has been some time since I last ventured so far north."

"I think," said Jane, working out her new way of speaking her mind, "that you are better suited here, Mr. Fitzwilliam. I can tell you are a man of town and not country; perhaps it is why it has been so long since you last ventured there in the first place."

If he did not get the hint, her point surely would have occurred to him from the reaction of his surrounding family members. His brother was nearly in hysterics while Darcy and his parents hid their smiles politely behind their napkins or spoonfuls of food. Lady Catherine was too busy attempting to observe her daughter down the table to have heard anything and so did not contribute.

In truth, Elizabeth and Anne had just discovered that Mr. Collins, the rectory of the de Bourghs' estate, was a distant relative of the Bennets' and they were wondering aloud at the coincidence when Lady Catherine decided to become involved:

"What are you saying, Anne?" she shouted across the table.

"I was just telling Miss Elizabeth how beautiful Rosings is in the spring," Anne said, her small voice barely carrying to her mother's ears.

"Well it is," Lady Catherine agreed gruffly. "It is a shame you shall never see it, Miss Elizabeth."

If that was the remark Elizabeth received when Lady Catherine knew nothing of her station or family, she did not wish to imagine what Lady Catherine's response would have been had she been made aware that her own clergyman was a relative.

"Pemberley is just as beautiful," Lady Fitzwilliam remarked, loud enough for it to carry where Lady Catherine's insult had gone, before capturing her attention once again. Whatever they had heard about Lady Fitzwilliam's gruffness was nothing in comparison to her sister-in-law. At least in the presence of Lady Catherine, Lady Fitzwilliam was an angel.

Elizabeth and Anne breathed a sigh of relief as soon as the woman's head was turned, safe again. Each had the same thought on their mind: whether or not they ever saw each other again, they had earned the other's utmost respect and friendship. If Lady Catherine had known her tormenting would have created this relationship, she may have endeavored to keep her mouth shut.

Supper was so successful that the girls went to the drawing room after dessert was served in high spirits. Lydia and Georgiana had had their first taste of fine public society and had been treated respectively by all their neighboring gentlemen and ladies. The cutthroat social etiquette of the entryway prior to sitting down for a meal had relaxed at the table and made for a more friendly experience. There was nothing that could be said at a supper table that could not be easily heard by everyone else; in a crowded room, however, it was difficult to associate rumors with their original circulator. It had only been Lady Catherine who had been bold enough, or inconsiderate enough, to display unruly behavior in the dining hall. It mattered little, however, as she had done no lasting harm. Those who knew her well knew what to expect, and those who had just met her, knew no different.

    Jane, whose evening started out precarious, was invited to play and sing first and did so admirably, a reflection of how her dinner had ended. For those who knew her before that evening's performance, it was like watching a caterpillar transform into a beautiful butterfly. She, who had always been beautiful, had come into her own, and knew herself.

    Later in the evening, when few were left besides those related, Georgiana, Elizabeth, and Lydia gave their "triplet" performance to which Lady Catherine could only remark upon how much Georgiana had improved while saying nothing of the Bennet girls' talents; something that all would have agreed was the kindest thing she'd done all evening.

    Halfway through the performances, Elizabeth heard Lady Catherine telling Darcy that he could expect a visit from her and Anne as long as they did not retire to the Fitzwilliams' estate, as was the current possibility.

    "I am not long either in town or in country, however, for a matter of my own estate calls me home sooner rather than later." She went onto explain that business with her clergyman required her attention, which captured that of Elizabeth. He had a new wife, she claimed, and he found it necessary to have her home to gauge her approval. "I shall see if he has taken my advice in finding a wife," she said, leaving Elizabeth to wonder what would happen if Lady Catherine sincerely disapproved. She giggled unexpectedly then, and coughed to cover it up.

"Are you alright, Miss Elizabeth?" asked Darcy kindly after confirming that his aunt was locked into conversation with Sir Fitzwilliam about their possible departure to the country.

It was an inappropriate thought that had prompted her laughter and so she blushed as furiously as she might have if her thoughts were found out. She secretly wondered how Darcy would respond if she told him the truth: that she had been curious as to whether or not Mr. Collins was holding out consummating his marriage until Lady Catherine returned home and approved of his choice of wife. Otherwise, if she did not approve, how was he expected to get rid of her?

She knew nothing of her cousin, Mr. Collins, other than what her mother had conjectured, which was not kind in the least. He was to inherit everything that was currently Mr. Bennet's and presumably send the unmarried Bennet girls out on the streets. This, however, had little to do with character, but if he really was seeking Lady Catherine's approval for his choice of wife, this did not recommend him too highly. Her mother, Elizabeth realized, would be furious that the man had married. After all, it was Mrs. Bennet's hope that she would be able to marry one of her daughters to the man so that she may keep their home. Elizabeth decided to write to her father of the news in the morning and instruct him to let her mother down easy.

"I am, thank you, Mr. Darcy. Something struck me as humorous and, not wishing to appear rude, you have only heard my attempts at covering my impromptu laughter."

"I am glad to hear that you are enjoying yourself and can only say that I hope it was not at my expense," he answered, smiling.

"Of course not, Mr. Darcy. You do not come off as a man who tolerates being laughed at, sir, and, even more so, as a man who does not give one reason to."

"I am glad I am not silly but I hope I am not as stern as you make me out to be."

"Stern –no. I have not found the word for you yet, Mr. Darcy."

"Can you so easily summarize a person in one word?" he asked, dying of curiosity at how she would answer.

"On occasion. Which is why I shall have to spend more time finding one for you, Mr. Darcy. Otherwise, you shall have to settle for several in most likely the same amount of time."

"Shall I reveal what my word or words for you in that same moment?"

She blushed, despite herself, forgetting for a moment that this was Mr. Darcy. In this room, this crowd, this evening, he seemed a normal gentleman, not someone whom she had spent an exorbitant amount of time with and, if it were any other gentleman –this *would have been* flirting. She let herself relax, give in to this moment of "would have been" and carried on as though he were always this charming, always this well dressed, mannered, and *new* to her.

"That would be most fair, I think, so long as our opinions were along the same lines with each other. It would not do for one to be complimentary while the other was harsh."

"Well, allow me to let you in on a little secret, Miss Elizabeth. If only one of us is to be complimentary, it will surely be me."

"I thank you ahead of time, Mr. Darcy."

"My opinion of you is a reflection of you, Miss Elizabeth. There is no need to thank me. Now, as you were the one to voice a hope in a imbalance of descriptions, it is clear to me that I must work hard to secure your regard."

"Don't be so hard on yourself, Mr. Darcy. One thing you should know about females is that if one is bold enough to compliment them, they will automatically think better of that person for their…shall we say, sign of good taste?"

"Ah, then…in case you forget this moment or any other that I have been kind, I insist that I go first when we reveal our words."

Elizabeth laughed loudly which, since nothing that they had said was spoken above a whisper, captured them quite an audience. "Oops," she whispered, turning red.

"Do not concern yourself. I like being the envy of every man in the room, having secured your attention this long and to have won a laugh from you."

Chapter 21

The memory of Darcy's words accompanied Elizabeth all the way home to the Darcy townhouse, visited her dreams, and were her companion at breakfast the following morning until the speaker himself joined her before the others arose, as was customary.

"Good morning, Miss Elizabeth. I trust you slept well after that long evening?" he said pleasantly, refilling her tea before getting his own.

"I did, Mr. Darcy. Thank you again for allowing my sisters and I to accompany you."

"It is not a matter of allowing, I would have begged if you had denied me the honor of your company. I am always hesitant to venture out into society, even when it is with those that I am related to. Colonel Fitzwilliam will have some stories for you, if you should want to know how difficult it is to get me out the door."

"There is no need to ask Colonel Fitzwilliam anything on the subject, Mr. Darcy, for he can only tell me what I wish to hear from you. And, in any case, I have no desire to hear how difficult you are to get out of the house, that, you can leave up to my imagination. I do, however, have a desire to hear *why* it is so difficult to get you out of the house –and hear it from *you*." She said this and dramatically crossed her arms when she finished, causing him to laugh.

"Oh?"

"What good is it to hear from a secondary source? They might be wrong. You –however, should not be wrong about yourself."

"I've been wrong about myself before and it is likely to happen again."

"I don't know if I agree with that. I don't think you have ever before acted knowingly against yourself –it is only that you saw a situation as one way, acted accordingly, and later were convinced to view it from another perspective."

"Have you not just proven me wrong again?"

"I have –but not about yourself. Now, if you will be so kind as to indulge me in why the Master of Pemberley is so rarely seen outside of his abode?"

"The short, simple answer would be that I am shy." He said it so matter-of-factly that she nearly laughed, thinking it was said in jest.

Lydia was right! Elizabeth realized when he did not, after too long, reveal he was joking. She was torn between astonished at Lydia's cleverness and disappointed in her own oblivion. She tried as best she could to relive every memory of hers with him to apply this perspective but could not make complete sense of it. There was a piece to the puzzle that was Mr. Darcy that she was missing, perhaps a few.

"I did not think of you as shy," she responded honestly.

"No, I did not guess that you would. Perhaps it started out as shyness and evolved into something less innocent –that is more likely. I am not the social butterfly that you undoubtedly have seen in my cousin, nor am I the confident, blossoming flower that you are, Miss Elizabeth." She nodded her thanks at the compliment and decided to dwell on it later. "I was shy, like Georgiana, and then when circumstances forced me out into society, when I assumed my role, I think this introversion altered when I became treated a certain way. There are not many outside my door, Miss Elizabeth, who treat me the way I would like to be treated. I am game to unmarried women, their mothers, their fathers...and to my family, I am a leader who is not allowed to fail, who is expected never to do wrong."

Elizabeth had never before seen anyone —not her parents or sisters, so genuinely and completely vulnerable as Mr. Darcy was in this moment. She was afraid to move —he spoke as though no one was there, as though it was all to himself. She did not wish to remind him of her presence, for she was petrified that it would embarrass him. It was not until he turned and their eyes met that she was sure he meant for her to hear it. She was not certain that he wouldn't regret her hearing it later, but she knew from the look in his large, reflective blue eyes, that he was at least certain *now*.

"Mr. Darcy, you are your own man. Separate from your family, distinct from your friends. You have the capacity to compel those around you to treat you the way you would like to be treated. If you remain silent —they will decide for you."

He blinked and looked at her as though seeing her for the first time. She suddenly felt completely exposed under his gaze, but the sensation was not unwelcome. His eyes were full of compassion, wonder, and…something she could not quite place. And, before she knew it, he was right in front of her. The proximity did not at all help her read the meaning of his look; in fact, the effect was the opposite. Her thoughts were scrambled, all explainable sensations evaporated, replaced by thrilling, baffling, and overwhelming ones. Before she could grasp what was happening, he closed the distance between them, clasped his warm, leathery hands behind her neck, and kissed her. It was charged, heated, and exhilarating. They could hear nothing but the sound of their own heavy breathing during the brief moments when their lips separated, want nothing more than to taste more of the other. They broke away when a clang from a fallen spoon jolted them back to reality.

"I am so sorry…" Darcy breathed. "I don't know…I don't know what came over me."

Elizabeth could make no answer —she had not even had time to give the moment a thought. It had all happened so fast, as though it may not have happened at all.

"It will not happen again, Miss Elizabeth," he said quickly. "You can trust me, I did not mean to betray your trust. I would never…"

The others, who said nothing of the tension in the room but instantly sensed that something was amiss, joined them at that moment. Darcy did his best to fall into his normal morning routine while Elizabeth chatted away unceasingly, faster than usual.

"You got more than what you bargained for, didn't you?" Colonel Fitzwilliam said, making Elizabeth pale. "Last night," he continued, calming her, "with my aunt, I mean."

"Oh!" Elizabeth nearly shouted. "She was not what I expected."

"No, she is a rare breed. A cross between bloodhound and royal, I believe," Colonel Fitzwilliam said above the protests of his cousins. "She makes my mother look the saint, god bless her. Miss Bennet, how was it having the unique honor of being cornered by such a lady for a good two hours?"

"As Elizabeth said, Lady Catherine was not at all what I would have expected from an aunt of yours. Your mother and father were very pleasant," Jane said simply, exercising her newfound honesty by leaving out any mention of Colonel Fitzwilliam's brother.

"And my brother?" he asked, too perceptive and too eager to ignore the subject entirely.

"If I found him half as charming as he found himself…" Jane began timidly, "then I would have liked him almost as much as I like you, Colonel." She finished strong amidst the laughter of those who were listening.

"Well spoken, my dear!" Colonel Fitzwilliam boomed. "I have half a mind to tell him. But don't worry!" he said, seeing the look on her face, "I will not, of course, but if I could…it would certainly humble him to a tolerable degree."

"Aunt Catherine was in rare form, William," observed Georgiana to her quiet brother. "I was very relieved at being seated down the table from her. But with the arrangements being switched, I was out of range of Anne also. You and Anne seemed to get along swimmingly, Elizabeth. I hope you found my cousin more inviting than my aunt."

"I did, thank you," replied Elizabeth. "Your cousin is a very pleasant lady. I must admit, I did not know what to expect of her after seeing Lady Catherine, but I came to like her a great deal once we were alone. The gentleman seated between us was an extraordinary creature, but I think we did alright despite his presence."

The ladies laughed, understanding exactly what Elizabeth meant while the gentlemen remained silent in their ignorance.

"We have not been allowed alone with Anne in nearly a decade, Miss Elizabeth," explained Richard, "ever since her father, Sir de Bourgh passed. She, who was quite a lively girl, is unrecognizable today under her mother's influence and abuse."

This saddened Elizabeth more than she could express and she sympathized with the obvious melancholy that Colonel Fitzwilliam's tone betrayed. "I feel very fortunate then," she said, "to have spent time with her away from her mother. If you should be so lucky, I think you will find that that Anne has not disappeared entirely. We spent a very pleasant evening together, she is as lively now as you say she was."

Colonel Fitzwilliam smiled widely but said nothing, lost in a daydream that Elizabeth had begun for him.

The gentlemen excused themselves after a while and retired to Darcy's study whilst the ladies organized themselves for a shopping trip. As it was their first legitimate outing for such a purpose, even Elizabeth was excited at the prospect of acquiring new bonnets, ribbons, gloves, and perhaps even a new dress. It had been so long since any of them had done such a thing that they all had many weeks' pocket money to spend and, for once, Elizabeth need not worry about purchasing books. Anything she had ever wanted to read was in one of Mr. Darcy's gigantic libraries.

The gentlemen, left to themselves, had more serious matters to discuss and deliberated for many an hour over whether or not Colonel Fitzwilliam would quit the service, a matter that one of last night's many discussions had spurred.

"I will think it over, as I have been known to do, another night. There are many a matters still, that weigh upon my mind," Colonel Fitzwilliam said, utterly fed up with the topic.

In truth, Darcy hardly cared to discuss it himself, but required something weighty to wrestle his mind away from the kiss…

"Richard, if it is a question of financials…" Darcy began, but was interrupted.

"It is, for once, not a matter of money. Allow me another night's sleep over it and with tomorrow's sun, will come my answer. Now on to you…was it my imagination, or did the ladies and I interrupt something between you and Miss Elizabeth this morning?"

"What?" Darcy said, buying time to think of something else to say. "You interrupted a discussion we were having about indecent relations, which of course you would know nothing about, but other than that… What do you mean?"

"I *mean* the lady was redder than an Egyptian sunset and you were stiffer than a board! If you would have been standing anymore upright, you would have fallen over!"

"You have let your imagination run wild cousin. Tell me, has it anything to do with seeing our aunt and cousin last evening?"

Richard turned nearly as red as he had accused Elizabeth of being in the breakfast room. "Absolutely not!"

"Then we have both let our speculation run away with us, haven't we?"

Richard said nothing. He was no longer willing to trade information to hear anything from Darcy. It wasn't worth it, in his mind, especially when he would most likely be able to figure out what, if anything, had occurred between his cousin and Miss Elizabeth in a matter of time.

That day's post had arrived hours before any of its recipients were available to look it over and, so, when the ladies arrived home with full shopping bags and empty pocket books, the gentleman were just sitting down to their mail.

"You have a letter here, addressed to all of you, and one specifically to Miss Elizabeth," said Colonel Fitzwilliam, sorting through it and finding his own.

"Ah, the infantry. Darcy!" he called down the hall, "I think I am being called back. So her majesty has decided the matter for me. Isn't that a funny thing?"

There was no reply and, seeing as how neither the Bennets nor Georgiana knew what he was referring to, they could only guess that Darcy's silence meant that he did not find whatever matter it was humorous.

Elizabeth was grateful that business kept Darcy in his study the majority of that day and that her own kept her happily distracted with her new purchases. It was not that she did not wish to see him –it was that she was not sure of how to behave when she did. She had hardly had time to think the matter of the morning over at all that day, being so caught up in her sisters' and Georgiana's conversations, and, in truth, she preferred it that way for she feared what she would conclude from it if she gave it too much thought. That night, she knew, would barely grant her any sleep, but at least for the day, she could ignore it.

While Georgiana and Lydia practiced a song from a new music book Georgiana had purchased and Jane diligently poured over a letter from their mother, Elizabeth did her best to pay attention to the one that she had received that day from her friend, Charlotte Lucas. She had not heard from Charlotte in nearly a month, so it was not lack of excitement keeping her fully engaged, but rather another questionable incident of the day and Elizabeth thought back on it to try and piece together what it could mean.

After careful deliberation, Elizabeth had decided that the majority of her pocket money would go to the ordering of two new dresses for her sorely outdated wardrobe. There was nothing like living amongst such fashionable society to make one feel too inadequate for any.

She thought she looked best in blue, so resolved to make at least one of her choices and resolved to pick the other after seeing the offered fabrics. It was when Georgiana suggested green that Elizabeth was forced to think back to the incident in the breakfast room.

"I highly suggest green, Lizzy," she had said, picking up a lovely deep shade of it and bringing it to her.

"Green?" she asked. Elizabeth owned one green dress but it was dull in comparison to whatever this fabric would create.

"Yes," she said, "my brother once remarked that you look very striking in green. It brings out your eyes." He had said as much, Georgiana reasoned, but at the time she did not think he meant it to mean more than a statement of fact. Since, of course, he had been careful to make any remarks about Elizabeth's physical appearance, good or bad, and this contributed to Georgiana's theory that her brother was half in love with her. He was far too self-conscious when it came to discussing her and may have been well on his way to expressing his feelings that morning in the breakfast room if they had not interfered.

Since this moment had been interrupted, Georgiana was determined to set things right and, since she was fairly certain that Elizabeth did not feel as strongly as her brother, wanted to pave the way for Elizabeth to open her mind (and heart) to the possibility. She watched Elizabeth carefully as she fingered the fabric, knowing there was much more to her thoughts than the color. She wanted Elizabeth to consider how she felt about Darcy preferring her a certain way. It was often, so far as Georgiana had ever heard, not until one was aware that they were being admired that the sentiment could be returned.

"That was kind of him," Elizabeth said, knowing nothing else to add. "I shall compare it to my other choices. Thank you, Georgiana."

It was half an hour later that Georgiana's efforts were rewarded when they left the dress shop where Elizabeth had made an order for two dresses: one blue and one green.

Her preoccupation in the sitting room was not due to being ungrateful for the compliment that Mr. Darcy had bestowed upon her, nor the honor of having a friend make a suggestion as to the type of dress she should order…it was just that she was at a loss to how she felt about it all. She was too conflicted to be flattered, too lost to be insulted, and too weary to be content. This chaos soon gave way to the warm, strong feeling of his lips, the taste of his breath, the feeling of his strong arms holding her, unnecessarily, against him. That kiss…

"I am married, Lizzy!" –the words caught her eye before she was completely lost in the memory of the kiss. *What?!* The letter she held in her shaking hands was directed *from* Charlotte Lucas and the writing surely belonged to the same woman, but the words did not –could not, belong to her. She scanned the paper desperately, blinking to hope that a clearer look would grant her a different sight.

"Charlotte is married!" Jane exclaimed from across the room, her reserve giving way to her shock and excitement.

"What?" demanded Lydia from the piano. "To who? While we are away? How could she already be married?"

"To none other than our cousin!" Jane continued in the same bold manner. "Why, this is preposterous!"

"Our cousin?" Lydia asked, at a complete loss as to whom Jane could mean.

"What does Charlotte say in her letter to you, Lizzy? Surely she explains the matter," Jane said, turning to Elizabeth who sat perfectly still in a stunned silence.

"I have only..." she could not explain that she was too distracted to read a letter that had been in her hands for nearly half an hour, "let me read it once again in order that I can properly explain. I hardly understand nor believe it myself." Elizabeth committed her full attention to the letter and read each new line with more despondence than the last.

"She has married Mr. Collins, who happened to have surprised Longbourn with a visit. Charlotte writes that it was his original intention to marry one of us, you, presumably, Jane," Elizabeth explained, "but that his attention quickly fell upon her in our absence."

"Mr. Collins? Who is to inherit..."

"Everything," said Elizabeth for her.

"Your estate is not tailored towards the female line?" asked Georgiana, stunned.

"Unfortunately not, and since our parents have no male heirs, the estate will fall to the next of kin. A rather distant relation, Mr. Collins, whom I found out last night is none other than your Aunt Catherine's rector."

"Rosings?" Georgiana asked in astonishment.

"Your cousin Anne and I discovered the coincidence last night. None of us has ever met Mr. Collins until now so I do not know what sort of man he is."

"To stand my aunt," Georgiana surmised, "he must either be a very patient sort of man or a very dull one."

"Is mother very furious?" Lydia asked of Jane.

"Unfortunately, it seems that way. She ends the letter recognizing that we will meet with better men in our present circumstance, however, so that is how she is deciding to deal with it."

"Then don't dare tell her that the three of us are further away from matrimony than when we set foot outside of Longbourn," Lydia joked.

"No," Jane said, laughing openly, "I will leave that fact out of my correspondence."

Georgiana contemplated the Bennets' predicament while her companions busied themselves penning letters home and to Charlotte Lucas in congratulations. Marriage was such a funny business to her now that she was grown. In her youth, it had seemed so romantic a prospect and, now, so controversial. It seemed to her, now that she was old enough to see how the world really worked, that hardly anyone married for love. It was a shame, she thought, but it made those that did even luckier. She would hold out for love, she decided. There was nothing else in the world she didn't have that she wanted or needed anyway. But love was something that could even evade the wealthy.

Chapter 22

The summer was beginning to dwindle, though this went vastly unrecognized except for the garden. The blooming months had gone and, with them, the lush leaves of the trees and brightness of the flowers. It would have taken a diligent pupil of gardening to perceive such a change yet, even those who remained unaware, could feel a slight change. There was a restlessness in the Darcy townhouse that could not be warded off by any ball, supper, shopping spree, or theatre show and the departure of Colonel Fitzwilliam who, despite Darcy's reasons voiced against his leaving, had answered the call to return to base, leaving a hole in everyone's heart and longing for new surroundings.

"We are to depart on the morrow, William," said Georgiana to her brother across their otherwise empty dinner table. The Bennet ladies had accepted the invitation to dine with the Gardiners on their last evening in town while the Darcy's remained at home to secure the remaining arrangements had been made. "It is official."

"And at no better time, I was beginning to acutely miss home."

"As was I. Town exhausts me so. Not only the marathon of social obligations we have seen to, but the pace of our surroundings. Everyone is in such a hurry here. In the country, we are allowed to breath."

"And deeply, for it smells much better there."

Georgiana could not laugh as heartily as she would have if she had not so much weighing on her mind. In all the weeks that had passed, she did not perceive a strengthening relationship between her brother and Elizabeth. She had cast aside her matchmaking duties, to be certain, but this had everything to do with seeing what her brother wanted and not anything to do with what she thought was best for him. She had begun to worry that he had resigned himself to marrying someone of a similar status after overhearing an argument he and her cousin had had before his departure.

"If I find myself at the doorstep of my parents' residence, it will not be for those reasons!" Richard's voice had too easily reached her ears from across the hall.

"You have missed the point of what I was saying," her brother had breathed.

"You want me to choose money over love. When this love would award me both, in all irony!" She could deny her interest no longer and, against her better judgment, had decided to listen at the door.

"It is irony that you hear only what you dislike! I've said that you should take your father up on his offer, take advantage of the opportunity to make money and, once you have, go to her."

"You make it sound so easy. What harm is there in making it on my own? You do not know the particulars of what my father has asked of me and I would be bald and crippled before I'd be making what I earn on my own now."

"You are an intelligent and business minded, I doubt that you would make less than you do now for even a year. If it is love –then it can wait, can it not?"

"You speak a lot of love for someone who claims to have little understanding of it. Love *can* wait, but not when it doesn't need to. You are attempting to delay my announcement in hopes that either she or I will find someone new."

"Excuse me, I thought I was speaking to my same cousin who, weeks earlier, was committed to having as much fun as he could before settling down with the richest woman that would have him, having sampled every type of love there is."

"You are a heartless bastard," she had heard her cousin grunt. "When I saw her..." his voice softened, before hardening once again, "Well, it is no matter! I am living out your creed, really. Marry at one's station or above –to one with an eerily similar upbringing, education, and social circle. Only, apart from your chilly way of putting things, it will include passion. So, it seems, your and my marriage will only differ in one way, but it is to be expected. You were always rather stiff, weren't you?"

"Insulting me won't get you anywhere. I will stand by you no matter what happens, I am not attempting to steer you away from what you want. You are too stubborn to be happy unless you do things your own way, so go..."

"Ah, I am exactly like you in that regard, aren't I?"

Georgiana had scurried away then, not wishing to risk being discovered by listening any longer. It was not the feud that had upset her, it was what her cousin had accused Darcy of saying of marriage.

"Brother," she said across the table at him. He looked up, knowing her tone meant that she wished to change the subject to something more serious. "This may seem to you rather out of nowhere, but it has concerned me of late. You will allow me to make my own match, won't you?"

He coughed up a mouthful of his soup into his napkin. "Uhh," he began, choking, "yes, Georgiana. I had not planned on arranging something for you. What has put that in your mind? You must find your own husband, Georgiana, for your chance at happiness."

"I am worried that you will not give yourself the same chance."

"What do you mean?"

"You want my happiness and I want yours. I hope that you will pick your wife for the same reasons that you hope I will look for in a husband. It is not a likeness of wealth or upbringing that will bring you happiness necessarily. I just hope, for once, you let your heart command you where so often your head gets in the way, William. You and I have been born with the gift of choice in our partners, we mustn't succumb to the restrictions of those around us —we must define our own. And love, at least I think, has no limitations, William."

Darcy stared at her a moment, in complete awe of the woman he saw before him where so often a little girl had sat before. She looked like their mother —*exactly* like their mother and, somehow, he could imagine those same words coming from his mother's mouth. For a moment, he could not tell if it was Anne or Georgiana speaking to him. They shared the same willful grace —they had as much power in their soft-spoken manner that many a warrior had in his war cry.

"Your advise is sound and appreciated, Georgiana, but please ease my mind by telling me why this is a sudden worry for you. It cannot be the impending presence of Miss Bingley?"

"It is not Miss Bingley, William, but it is the dozens like her on my mind. I..." she could not put into words what she wanted without specifically naming Elizabeth. She knew, she had seen with her own eyes how he looked at her. As much as he might deny it and as much as she remained oblivious, it was undeniable. All that had been her aim was to tell him that she would approve and to encourage him.

"Yes?"

She could not bring herself to say it. She thought he would have been further along at it than this, surely thought he would guess at where this was leading. *But men are slow!* Georgiana decided. There was no use bringing it up now, it might only serve to scare him off. If he were told that his interest was not as secretive as he thought, he might back off completely.

"Just follow your heart, William. And do me a favor: if a gentleman is half in love with me, do let me know, for I see that he will take an eternity to admit it to me and a lifetime to even admit it to himself."

Chapter 23

The carriages peeled away, packed as two could be. Georgiana and Lydia had opted to ride with the Gardiners, leaving Mr. Darcy alone with the eldest Bennet girls and a carriage-full of their belongings.

"With all the shopping you've done," he said to Jane and Elizabeth as they started off, "we'll be lucky to make twice their time."

"You can't fault us for wishing to look fashionable in your company, Mr. Darcy," Elizabeth teased. The awkwardness that their kiss had caused had all but dissipated as a result of spending an enormous amount of time together. If they had not been living under the same roof, both owned, they most likely would have never spoken again. As it was, Darcy could only claim to be held up in his study with work for three days afterwards and, after, was dragged out by his sister who insisted that all work could wait until Pemberley. Their association was forced at best and later resorted to their old understanding as though nothing had occurred at all.

The kiss had troubled Darcy a great deal as he could still not explain what had come over him and impelled him to do it. He went so far in his musings at one time to say that he had had no part of it at all. Along with the impulse to do it, the passion that exploded once he had was also inexplicable. He had never felt anything like it, never imagined he would and, as much as he wished to deny it, he could not regret it. It had been too good a feeling to ever do so.

Elizabeth recounted one of her sister Mary's many reflections on the subject of passion many a time to explain what had occurred between them and what had induced Mr.

Darcy to do such a thing. Mary would have told her that people, men especially, were governed by impulses and were only the measure of how much they could control them. This meant that Darcy had, in a sense, lost control for a moment, and could only be blamed with being human. But not everything was so black and white as her sister liked to believe. The look he had given her before he did it...she could make it appear before her in her daydreams as if it were really he staring at her that way again. She recounted more often than she ought and had begun to dismiss it of late as easily as she had recalled it, finding that the memory stirred up many of those bewildering feelings that she had felt when his mouth was pushed against hers.

It was a kiss, Darcy often thought to himself, *just a kiss —and not one that was meant to mean anything —why would it be?* These were the thoughts that had kept Darcy up at night and these were the sleepless nights that had left him particularly longing his bed at Pemberley. As Jane and Elizabeth laughed in the coach on the bench across from him, he wondered if Elizabeth had preferred her bed in town or at Pemberley. *Or perhaps she'd prefer mine.*

"Sorry," he said aloud and straight to the subject of his preoccupation.

"Sorry?" Elizabeth asked, puzzled.

"Oh," he said, embarrassed, "I thought I stepped on your foot when I shifted."

"My feet are safe, Mr. Darcy. Your coach, I think, is too large to allow that possibility."

She was right, he saw. The floor separating the benches was enormous and would not possibly allow him to shift and step on her foot. His embarrassment grew and he quieted again, determined not to have another outburst. To take his mind off of her, he internally listed off all the things that needed to be attended to once they arrived home. *Check the books, promote a chef's assistant, repaint the green walls of the east sitting room...green...*" His gaze was arrested by Elizabeth's green dress; new, as far as he could tell. He let the curves and folds of it take him upwards towards her eyes and did not look away until she caught him staring. Caught, he looked quickly downwards and wrestled a book from his bag, finding it necessary to busy his mind in another fashion.

Elizabeth did her best to return to the conversation she was having with Jane who had been too busy gazing out the window to notice what had transpired. She did not let the small smile escape though there was little she could do about the rosiness of her cheeks at the moment. *Flattered* would not have been the right word and she would have been offended were there anyone in the vicinity to suggest it. It was simply that in the process of choosing what she would wear on their travels earlier that morning, she had imagined something of the kind happening. Not that she gave Mr. Darcy's opinion or approval any thought at any point during the day –no. She reasoned it was just in this case as Georgiana had so gotten the matter stuck in her head.

There would not be a time, Elizabeth feared, in the near future that she would be able to don this green dress without first thinking of Mr. Darcy. It was of no consequence, she affirmed, that she had worn this dress more than any other since receiving it, but for this she had a perfectly sound explanation: Georgiana had good taste, and Elizabeth thought she might look better in it rather than it the blue one as she had originally surmised. No, it was not her usual custom to concern herself particularly with her appearance but, lately, something had come over her and she found herself taking a bit longer to ready herself in the morning, stealing more glances in the mirror. It was a natural phase, of course, a natural part of growing up. Though, if she had had a handmaid to wait on her in the morning, such a woman might have intimated that she spent more time getting ready when she knew the master would be present that day. Luckily for

Elizabeth Bennet, she needn't worry about having a handmaid and so was left in blissful ignorance of this fact.

"This is too beautiful!" Jane exclaimed when their carriages plunged into the thick of the wooded wild that made up the outskirts of Lambton and Pemberley.

"I am proud to call this place my home, it was a pleasure growing up in the country," Mr. Darcy said to her, "As I am sure you well know."

"I do —but your home's surroundings are much more lush than ours. This is incredible. I had no idea the north of England would be so splendid. Lizzy, you must have been in heaven walking here."

"I was," Elizabeth answered, laughing at how well her sister knew her.

"I can attest to that, Miss Bennet. She could put my horse to shame, the miles she roamed here for a mere matter of weeks." This last statement was focused primarily on Elizabeth, and Darcy's eyes shone with admiration such that he was before too uptight, too in control to betray. It had been a long carriage ride, a long day, and the sight of these all-too-familiar woods against Elizabeth's tanned skin and hazel eyes drove the sense right out of him. He was too exhausted to recognize that in his carelessness, he may have admitted his tenderness for her to himself or even the lady in question and this would not do. "I must advise you not to give into your desire for such an adventure as soon as we arrive, Miss Elizabeth, for I would not feel comfortable knowing you would so easily blend into the forest in that magnificent dress. As your host, I could not allow it."

"You so easily guessed my train of thought!" Elizabeth exclaimed, too invigorated by the sight of trees and too energized by his teasing to think too much about his compliment or his direct attentions.

"Guess –no. Read, more like it. Your eyes bulged as soon we were surrounded by woods, like a kid in a candy shop."

Elizabeth could make no answer but could only lean on Jane, overcome by a violent bout of laughter. It was not long before Jane and Darcy made eye contact and were driven to the same circumstances, doubled over and heaving. Elizabeth, who had begun first, was the first to clear her throat and finally manage to say, "eyes bulged?" before collapsing into a renewed fit of giggles, wiping the tears from her eyes.

Many minutes went by before Darcy gained enough control over himself to sit up and look out the window, breathing heavily between an explanation that they were just coming up the drive. "If you ladies had your new hats in the car of this carriage, I'd say that we succumbed to the glue!" he said of their overwhelming fit.

The three hysterical passengers of the second coach were the subject of every servant's discussion in the Darcy household that night; every man and woman alike determined to spread the news that their master was the image of his old self and that, at least in hushed whispers it was suggested, one of the ladies in that carriage had something to do with his miraculous transformation. With the news that the Bingley's would join them on the morrow, this rumor was particularly encouraging, as it somewhat diminished the possibility of seeing Miss Caroline Bingley as Mistress of Pemberley.

Chapter 24

"My dear, Miss Darcy, you are a lady! Why, Mr. Darcy! How did you ever let this happen? The young Miss Darcy and I got along quite splendidly and now I shall have to do everything in my power to see that this grown up Miss Darcy is partial to me!" Miss Caroline Bingley spoke to Darcy about his sister as though there were not seven other people in the room and even ignored Miss Darcy, though it was about her that she spoke.

In truth, she played to the audience she wished to be the real one: Mr. Darcy and *only* Mr. Darcy. Her brother, Georgiana, the Gardiners, and Bennet girls were all left on either side of him to admire her boldness and decide whether or not they were glad of her piercing eyes and sharp voice not focusing on them.

"It was only a matter of time," Darcy said all too politely for both his sister and Elizabeth's liking.

"It seems I had very little left to do but grow, Miss Bingley. It is very nice to see you again. I hope you and Mr. Bingley will feel as though you are home as long as you remain here. I urge you not to hesitate to let me know if there is anything you require."

Darcy admired the way that his sister had come to steer the conversation to a land of relevance and appropriateness. He also did not mind that when she spoke, he no longer needed to. There was such pressure in certain company and he could hardly stand speaking in front of Miss Bingley any longer.

He was ashamed to admit that he had appreciated her company when they had first met. To someone feeling irreparably shy and like an outcast, her conceited air and pretentious comments felt welcoming. It was as though their assumed sense of pride could protect him. It had, at least, awarded him a safe circle of friends. But safe, as he had learned recently with his sister, did not mean happy. And as he had come to realize about himself —safety would not make him happy either.

Perhaps, he thought as Miss Bingley went on about how long it had been since she had last set foot at Pemberley, *if I had extended my social circle beyond the Bingley's, I would have met someone like the Gardiners, like the Bennets, like…no…*as his gaze drifted from Caroline Bingley to the second eldest Bennet sister, he realized that, no matter how long or far he looked, he would never again meet anyone like Miss Elizabeth Bennet.

"Allow me to introduce you to our other guests, Mr. Bingley, Miss Bingley," Georgiana cut in as soon as she was afforded the opportunity. She listed off the occupants of the entry room and, without much sarcasm; Miss Bingley greeted them in turn.

The lady's brother, Elizabeth observed, could not be more different than his sister. He was genial, bright-eyed, and high-spirited. She was excited to see how well he would impact the group despite his sister's negative qualities. Elizabeth decided to keep an open mind since her arrogance reminded her so much of Darcy's behavior when they had first met. Perhaps her vanity, too, would melt away once they got to know each other. When the gentleman separated (Mr. Gardiner included, once the easygoing Mr. Bingley insisted that he join the business discussions in Darcy's study), the ladies were led into the garden-facing sitting room and were treated to tea and sandwiches, something that Georgiana had arranged.

"It is early for tea, don't you think?" Miss Bingley leveled at them as Mrs. Reynolds poured, looking first at Mrs.

Gardiner and then at the Bennets in turn to locate which of them would be most appropriate to take her side. She could sense that they were unfashionable, but knew not how much so as their very presence countered that assumption. She settled on Lydia, deciding that her youth would render her more pliable to her control.

"I did not think you'd mind it, Miss Bingley, after your journey. We enjoyed a particularly early and light breakfast this morning, so I thought it might work best for all of us." Georgiana said this all managing to hide the feeling of embarrassment or shame. Only she could detect the slight shakiness of her voice, but even this relaxed as she spoke on. By the end of it, she felt almost as if there was nothing she couldn't say to anyone deserving in the presence of the Bennets and Mrs. Gardiner. "Thank you, Mrs. Reynolds," Georgiana said to the housekeeper, dismissing her just after clearing her of any of Miss Bingley's blame.

"Of course, Miss Darcy," Mrs. Reynolds said, bowing and smiling a bit larger than her usual custom. If she had been indebted to Miss Elizabeth Bennet for the change in Georgiana when she had first come to Pemberley, it was nothing to what she was grateful to the lady for now. She left, taking one more glance at Miss Bingley's ghostly-white face, knowing that the household staff's nerves could need nothing more than a description of what had just occurred to make their day.

"Of course, I had only meant to express my surprise at the impeccable timing. One's stomach cannot always be dictated by social expectation and etiquette," Miss Bingley said quickly.

To everyone's relief, this chagrin rendered her silent for nearly an hour while the others spoke of their journey to Pemberley.

"This setting tempts me to become a good a walker as Elizabeth," Jane said.

"Until a time as we are so accomplished, I might suggest that we take horses out to explore the landscape. There is a beautiful path along the creek that was a favorite of my father's," Georgiana answered.

"Might I suggest that all but Elizabeth are given horses? She surely doesn't need one," remarked Lydia in good humor.

"I cannot possibly live up to the myth you have created for me!" Elizabeth exclaimed.

"An exploration of the grounds, I think, will be great fun. And I shall have a picnic packed for us as well so that we may venture as far as is possible. Mrs. Gardiner, might we beg you a tour of Lambton when we go into town? I am eager to know how it was when my mother was alive."

"Of course, Miss Darcy, it would be my pleasure."

"Were you well acquainted with the late Mrs. Darcy?" Miss Bingley asked, perking up at the possibility of learning how these people had become acquainted with the Darcy's.

Mrs. Gardiner began her short explanation of having grown up in Lambton and belonging to a similar circle of Mrs. Darcy lacking any pretention that Miss Bingley might have expected from such a story.

"It is a marvelous coincidence, you see," Georgiana jumped in, "for I met Elizabeth by chance in town and we became instant friends. She joined me at Pemberley about two months ago now, though it is hard to believe that such a time has gone by already, where we were joined by Miss Lydia. Circumstances drove us back to town and there we were met by the Gardiners and Miss Bennet."

"Have you any other relatives, Miss Elizabeth? We should undoubtedly alert the household of their arrival," Miss Bingley leveled at Elizabeth, acknowledging her to potentially pose the biggest threat. Jane, the eldest, was certainly striking, but it was Elizabeth that had garnered the most time with Mr. and Miss Darcy. If there was one thing Mr. Darcy would used to, it was a pretty face; Jane Bennet was nothing out of the ordinary. But Elizabeth's estimation she was still unsure of.

"My father, mother, and two younger sisters will remain safely at home for the time being," Elizabeth said, laughing gaily afterwards, finding no reason yet to be particularly offended. She was aware that she had been chosen as a target, but as there was nothing she needed or wanted from Miss Bingley, there was no reason to be irked. "The household would undoubtedly need to be warned in such a circumstance, however."

Miss Bingley did not at all appreciate Elizabeth's ability to laugh at herself, to have turned her masked insult into something to be laughed about. It depreciated one's worth, to be sure, to turn an affront into a joke; it was practically admitting that it was true.

"Your parents must be relieved at having three daughters out of the house for so long," she remarked.

"Not as relieved as I am grateful that they have agreed to part with them for so long," Georgiana cut in.

Miss Bingley's look soured and she quieted again, unable to raise conflict with Mr. Darcy's sister, no matter how much she may have deserved it. Miss Darcy had changed a great deal since last she saw her, and it was no doubt due to these Bennet girls' poor influence. Since these girls had such a tight hold on her, there would be nothing that Miss Bingley could do directly to cut them out. She would focus her energy on Mr. Darcy. He, surely, would be made to see how negative of an influence these people had on his sister. Georgiana Darcy was practically out; there was no excuse to have such abysmal company about her. It would no doubt injure her marriage prospects.

Though the ladies did rather well taking into consideration the presence of Miss Bingley, it was easily stated that the gentlemen enjoyed their day far more. The study was rife with good humor and, though they did not need him, Darcy found himself acutely missing Colonel Fitzwilliam, recognizing that he would have adored this meeting. What began as Bingley detailing the houses he had toured became a hilarious discussion of construction mishaps. Only one of the homes that Bingley had seen was presently available to live in –the others would need months of work after purchase before they even resembled an estate.

"This last one, Darcy, why –I almost burst into laughter in your entryway earlier while Caroline was going on about it – the one not but five miles from here, it is scarcely more than a pile of wood and bricks."

"A fire, was it?" asked Darcy.

"Yes, but it was the attempted rebuilding that did the rest of the damage. The gentleman who lived in it when it was burnt down decided on a shoddy contractor to build it back up cheap and they managed to outdo the fire in damages."

"It can't be *that* bad," Mr. Gardiner said, laughing.

"We could take horses there tomorrow, if you don't believe me. But if you two went alone…you would easily ride past it and complain to someone nearby that they needed to see to their pile of trash."

The resounding laughter gave way to Darcy clearing his throat and asking what his intentions were.

"Well, I quite liked the livable one I saw, Netherfield. Though it may have been my falsified perspective that warmed the place up to me. After all, any place with a roof would have been easily recommendable to me."

"Netherfield? That was the one south, was it?" asked Darcy.

"Near the town of Meryton," Bingley answered.

"Meryton? What a coincidence!" Mr. Gardiner exclaimed. "That is where my nieces are from. I have probably driven past that estate, sir. If I am thinking of the correct one, it is just opposite to the town of my sister's home."

"That is a wonder!" Bingley remarked.

"And if so, it does have a nice roof!" Mr. Gardiner said before the discussion dissolved into bouts of laughter once again.

"If it weren't for the prospect of seeing the property close to you, Darce, I would have rented out for a trial period. Caroline wouldn't have protested too much, but of course we had to come here."

"So you'll let Netherfield it sounds like?" Darcy clarified.

"I don't see why not, seeing as how we're now familiar with the some of our neighbors. What kind of place is Meryton, Mr. Gardiner?"

"I have not spent too much time there, you must remember," Mr. Gardiner explained, "but it is not a place that takes a long time to get to know. It is a simple place, full of welcoming people. You would find the estate quiet for the most part, the neighbors would most likely visit to pay a respectful greeting to you and go about their business. It is a friendly place, but not a social place as you might be used to. People keep to their own. If the country is what you wish for, the country is what you'll get. But, I must add, it is not as lush as the parts around here."

"No, I know what you mean. I am a social man, I must admit, and though keeping my townhome would mean giving me the opportunity to leave the country whenever I wished, it is difficult for me to imagine living in such a way. Caroline, too, would want to host."

"The point of owning a country estate is to bring people to you," Darcy explained. "To get away from town –but bring half of town with you. Caroline will have no want of society and you will have no want of company."

"An idea occurred to me on the way here, Darcy, that I know you will not like," Bingley admitted jovially which struck Mr. Gardiner as funny.

"Oh?"

"Until a time such that a place I adore, in my budget, makes itself available to me —I believe I will spend time out of town letting country estates." He held up his hand when Darcy tried to protest. "I know that you want me to establish something for my family name and children —but, I see nothing wrong in allowing my son the same honor if nothing catches my eye. I will always have a home in London and I will always designate homes outside of it. It will be the same as having a country estate, only I will never know exactly where mine is or will be at any given moment. I think it suits me better anyway. You know I was never much one to stay in one place. I am a bit," he added to Mr. Gardiner alone, "...what did your cousin used to say about me, Darcy?"

"Flighty," said Darcy dismissively and fell into deep reflection while Bingley and Mr. Gardiner talked. He would have argued vehemently against Bingley's decision if it weren't for one statement: *"I think it suits me better anyway."* This left Darcy unable to clear his head of the conversation he had had with his cousin, sister, and Elizabeth on this very same topic.

"If Lydia were to always wish to run away with the circus, I might make better use of my time ensuring that she found appointment with the circus safely rather than trying to talk her out of it," Elizabeth had said. If this was what Bingley wanted —Darcy would need to support him and see to it that he went about this venture in the most intelligent way possible. He could see Bingley's eyes nervously flicking back between his conversation with Mr. Gardiner and himself, as though he were nervous of what Darcy would say of his admission. *And with good reason,* Darcy realized. He had never given credit to anything Bingley had said he had wanted before. Sure, he had steered him away from some real mistakes over the years, but he had also managed to steer him away from things that he had had no right to.

He had always justified his actions in two ways. The first, that he only had the best intentions. The second, that if he was really suggesting something that Bingley did not want to do –Bingley simply wouldn't have done it. He was sure that, deep down, Bingley knew that Darcy had been right about everything, and perhaps he had. But it was time to let go. Bingley would only learn now from his own mistakes and need to know to correct them on his own. He felt a tremendous weight lift off his shoulders and he spoke then without thinking, interrupting his guests slightly:

"I think it does suit you better, Bingley. Netherfield might be the perfect place to begin, if you still think you'd like it. Otherwise, the market of rentals will open more options to you, as before you were only looking to purchase."

Bingley's eyes lit up in surprise and he answered him eagerly, "Netherfield will do find for now, I cannot think of stomaching another bout of tours! It was amusing for the first...three houses and then it grew more than tedious. I will write to the man at Netherfield, but I might take a day or two more to think it over."

"Good idea," Darcy said and, seeing the look of sheer appreciation in Bingley's eyes, he knew that he had done right by his friend –and also acknowledged what a great disservice he had done him thus far. If he had had the foresight to trust in Bingley –to listen to him before– his friend may have come a long way (his *own* way), much faster.

Chapter 25

Darcy regrettably was detained by business while the others spent the next two days touring the grounds, picnicking, and venturing to Lambton. Both Bingley and Mr. Gardiner kindly offered to stay back and help, but Darcy, knowing that they would both rather be out with the ladies, begged them off. The quiet after so long spent in company was not as welcoming as he thought it might be —not as comforting as it used to. *Now that I know and like what I'm missing,* Darcy realized. He resolved to steal a moment alone with his sister to see how she was doing with Miss Bingley thus far for, up until then; they had not yet been able to secure audience with the other.

On the second day, Darcy found his desk was piled with more somehow than the day previous and so resolved to ask that Bingley and Gardiner stay back for at least part of the morning to help him. He had never before asked for help, but this was something he felt that the *new, more learned Darcy* should do. If not, he could risk the possibility of joining them at the lakes and if all that stood between his freedom and his deterrence, Georgiana would be furious if he did not take advantage of the assistance that was offered. And, he openly admitted, he could use the company.

"William?" Georgiana said, knocking on her brother's study door. He called for her to enter, chuckling about her tracking him down first.

"Supper is almost ready but I told Mrs. Reynolds I'd get you."

"I am glad, I was going to steal you a moment this evening as it is, as I am afraid I am going to steal your two gentlemen companions tomorrow to help me with my work."

"You're going to allow Mr. Bingley and Mr. Gardiner to help you?" She was as surprised as she was pleased, leaving him conflicted also, not knowing whether to be disappointed in his past behavior or proud of his new conduct. He decided, as he often found himself doing these days, putting Elizabeth's advice into practice. Something his sister had repeated to him: *"dwell on the past as it gives you pleasure, but to dwell at all denies us the present and risks our future."*

"I am, Georgie. Mr. Gardiner is an upstanding businessman and I could use his insight. I know that I have more experience than Bingley in such matters, but there are things he undoubtedly learned from his father that could be of use to me and I always appreciate his opinion."

"That is wonderful, Will. I certainly don't mind, but I think Bingley might, despite his eagerness to help you."

"Oh?"

"If I have eyes at all, it appears to me that he would mind leaving the side of a certain lady."

Not Elizabeth! It felt as though someone had poured cold water over him. His mind instantly retrieved the memory of dinner they had all shared the night before —she had laughed at him, he—at her. He could envision them walking arm and arm towards their picnic, laughing easily, jovially…not a care in the world.

"But perhaps it's a passing fancy," Georgiana said. "After all, he hasn't known Jane for that long. But as they so often say…*love at first sight*…"

"Jane?!" he demanded, as though furious she would suggest that anyone could like anyone besides Elizabeth.

"Yes, Jane. He is smitten, to say the least, and Caroline is throwing every insult at Elizabeth and completely ignoring the trouble that her brother is getting himself into. It's all very strange, Will. I am very glad that Bingley is here and there is no reason he and Jane should not like one another and perhaps let it develop into something more, but Caroline's behavior is beyond my comprehension."

"Elizabeth?" *Why would Caroline be mean to Elizabeth?*"

"Yes, Bingley likes Jane and Caroline hates Elizabeth."

"Do I need to tell her to leave?"

"Absolutely not, it is nothing the lady can't handle herself. I think she finds it amusing, actually. I try to quiet Caroline as often as I can. Jealousy is certainly a factor. Do you think Jane and Mr. Bingley would make a good pair?"

He could not address the question at hand because it was the furthest thing from his mind.

"You probably don't care anyway —what did you want to see me about?" she asked after a while of silence.

"Sorry, Georgiana, I am distracted."

"I know, you have work on your mind."

"Nothing more important than what you have to say, my dear. I simply wished to hear your visit was unfolding."

"Swimmingly, even considering Caroline's attempts to thwart it. Bingley is very pleasant company. I only wish Richard was here."

"I was thinking the same. I hope that, if it is as you say, Bingley is acting a gentleman with Miss Bennet."

"Of course he is. I believe the lady is unaware; the gentleman himself may be unaware for all my understanding of love. It is only the outside observers that suspect anything so far."

Though he could not bring himself to say it, Darcy wanted a wealthier woman for his friend to further secure his late father's holdings. Bingley's earnings were no means precarious, but a well-endowed match would guarantee that Bingley would never have to set foot back in trade. Of course he did not know the Bennets' income, but he could assume that, without a home in town and with relatives like the Gardiners (as fashionable as they were for members of trade), they could not be as wealthy as would suit. He recalled his conversation, then, he had had with his cousin, fully realizing the irony of the upper classes only marrying into those of their status. Wealth upon wealth was all that was gained, while those who stood to benefit were ignored.

Even if Darcy married someone outside the same earnings pool as he, there would be a great backlash despite his complete lack of need for financial gain. Perhaps his cousin was right —the greatest blessing of the wealthy classes might be the freedom to choose a spouse, of any social standing. Though no one seemed to recognize or practice it.

"Your understanding of love?" he asked, wishing to understand what Georgiana had meant by it.

"It is limited, I am afraid, to gentlemen not recognizing that they're in love, ladies who do not know they are the object or target of it and are consequently not even given the chance to bask in it or decide whether or not it is returned."

"Gentlemen?"

"Yes. William. Plural, gentlemen."

She knew he would ask nothing further and feared that neither would he understand further. The case with Mr. Bingley was exactly what she saw with her own brother: a man in love who could neither admit it to himself or to the lady in question. If Jane returned Mr. Bingley's feelings, Georgiana could not yet perceive it. But she wondered if Jane were more likely to if she knew that the gentleman favored her. After all, who was brave enough to host feelings for someone when they could not easily see that it would be returned? Jane was too modest, surely, to perceive that Mr. Bingley liked her and would chalk it up to his being a very attentive gentleman. Georgiana resolved to speak to Elizabeth about her, for surely she would have perceived Bingley's regard. Something must be done so that Mr. Bingley's love did not die before it was given the opportunity to be requited.

"You're not playing the matchmaker?" Darcy asked, still puzzling out what his sister had said. Georgiana moaned, recognizing that he had no understanding of what she meant. He could not possibly think his regard for Elizabeth was so secretive. Even Miss Bingley, she began to suspect, could perceive it, and she had only just arrived.

"I am not, William. Pemberley doesn't need a matchmaker, it needs a miracle worker."

Chapter 25

"I am sold on Netherfield! I wrote to the lawyer yesterday," Bingley triumphantly announced in Darcy's study.

"Congratulations, Mr. Bingley," said Mr. Gardiner, overlooking Mr. Darcy's plans for excavating part of the river as he had arrived and begun working an hour before Bingley.

Darcy, was slower to react, processing how he *should* feel for his friend rather than what he felt for himself at the moment.

"How exciting, Bingley," he finally answered, smiling and getting a large one in return.

If his sister was correct, this decision may have had more to do with Jane Bennet than Netherfield itself. *But,* he reminded himself, *either way, I am to support him.*

"I hope you will join us, Darcy. It is the tentative plan at the moment to ride with the Bennets down once we have worn out our welcome with you."

"What a splendid idea," remarked Mr. Gardiner.

"He says so," Bingley said to Darcy of Mr. Gardiner, "but he has already refused my invitation so I am not going to easily believe that he thinks it's a *splendid idea* after all."

"Refused is a strong word," Mr. Gardiner said, laughing and, looking at Darcy, explained, "I simply said that I would have to see if I can again be away from my business for so long. It would be marvelous to see my sister and my other nieces, so I only hope that I can give Mr. Bingley a 'yes.'"

Darcy marveled at how close Bingley and Mr. Gardiner had grown in the past couple of days. After all, they had only just met. It was curious, he thought, that you can know one person for a lifetime and not be as close as you get to someone you come by in passing. What he saw between Mr. Gardiner and Bingley was like an uncle's care for a nephew and he could not deny feeling that way about his relationship to Mr. Gardiner either. He was something between a mentor and an equal, something near family. *What had Elizabeth said about choosing friends to make your family?*

As the following day would bring them to the Lakes, the ladies set about enjoying a quiet day. Miss Bingley had calmed considerably, Georgiana had noted, with such a prolonged absence from Darcy. There was hardly any point in belittling competition when the prize was not there to witness it.

Miss Bingley's forced kindness got her all the information she needed, she thought, and covertly, she believed also. And, without being privy to Mr. Darcy's behavior towards any of them, she relaxed, knowing that neither the Bennets nor Gardiners posed any threat —how could they, after all, with how low they were? Every worry she held before they had described away with their low connections, their education, and their links to trade. She had an overactive imagination, she reasoned. Mr. Darcy could never align himself with such persons, even if he had for a moment considered it.

"I will venture out for one more walk this afternoon while the sun is warm," Elizabeth said.

"You are some walker, Miss Elizabeth," Caroline observed, looking to the others for assistance in any disparaging that might be done.

"If she should set out now, I imagine she would beat us to the lakes," Lydia said.

"So long as that is not your aim, Lizzy, I will join you," Georgiana said.

Elizabeth laughed and, taking her arm, led the way outside, leaving the other ladies behind.

"I have a confession," Georgiana revealed when they were not three yards from the house.

"Is it that we're setting out for the lakes on foot?" Elizabeth asked.

"Not exactly..." said Georgiana. "I had a theory that I wished to know if you shared. Mr. Bingley, if I know anything about gentlemen, is particular to Jane. Would you agree?"

"I would," Elizabeth said. "As good a man as Mr. Bingley is, I admit that it concerns me slightly. Jane, as beautiful as she is, has had her fair share of suitors, but none that could stay constant."

"That is very strange, I think. What do you think it was?"

"At first, I thought it was her lack of connections as she has always been too sweet, beautiful, and kind to blame. But now, upon careful reflection, I think it may have been the men's vanity. She is so shy, you see, that it is sometimes difficult to see how she feels. Perhaps her suitors feared she was disinterested and fled before their pride was injured rather than take the risk. But in that, I hold to the men not being worth her so long as they were unwilling to take a chance."

"It must be so, for no fault can lie with her. Do you think Bingley would be a good match for her?"

"I do. Their personalities will do well for each other; his joviality will bring her out of her shell, absolutely. And she might teach him some regulation. She likes him, to be sure. Though I am not sure she is yet willing to admit it."

"She likes him?"

"I was afraid that you could not have noticed. I hope it is not the same for her as with the other gentlemen. Though, even this time, it's different. I can see her regard more clearly than before. It is possible that she cares for him already more than she did for any of the others."

"But, Elizabeth...as much as I do not wish to think it, what if Bingley sheds his feelings once his attentions aren't returned equal enough in his mind? Surely he is the most well intentioned suitor, is he not?"

"He is, and I fear it also. Perhaps I should speak to her. I do not know whether she holds the same fears as he, afraid of showing feelings that may not be returned, or if it is her shyness that she is letting get a hold of her. Either way, I know that her heart is touched and I would not wish her to be injured when it can be so easily remedied and her happiness secured."

"I only wish to see both Jane and Mr. Bingley happy, Elizabeth. Now, of your own experience..." Georgiana put together her phrasing very carefully, "...do you ever think that you could be the object of someone's affections and not realize it?"

"I pride myself on being an observer of people, Anna, but of course I cannot expect that I have perfected my skills in only under twenty years. I believe that it could happen, either in ignorance, misunderstanding, extreme humbleness (meaning that it is difficult to imagine being the object of someone's gaze), and perhaps when the feelings are mutually felt and therefore are delicate at best, subject to all sorts of feelings of diffidence."

"I think that the regard is mutual in Jane and Bingley's case, only that one of them is poor at hiding his feelings but that Jane is too unassuming to perceive them. We have to talk with her, Elizabeth. I could not stand to see either of their heart's broken. And," she added, "one more thing, Lizzy. You must promise me that if you perceive such a case with me in the future —if I am so blind and stubborn as to not perceive a gentleman in love with me or, even worse, if I am so ignorant as to not acknowledge that I am in love, shake me until I am made to understand it."

Elizabeth laughed at her friend's grave tone for such a silly topic and laughed harder when Georgiana did not join her.

"Why are you so serious, Georgiana? All will be well —it is love, after all. It is supposed to be a wonderful thing. I suppose I should have said that you have the same responsibility to me —to let me know if I am half in love with a man and will not yet admit it." She rolled her eyes, knowing that it could never happen.

"I cannot promise such a thing, Elizabeth, for I believe it is too late."

They had reached the door to the sitting room by then and rejoined the ladies, never allowing Elizabeth clarification on what Georgiana had meant.

Chapter 26

Mrs. Gardiner's descriptive praise of the lakes did not fall short of the beauty that managed to quiet them all. The party had enjoyed a boisterous journey north, stopping on occasion to enjoy various sites, picnic, and switch seats to secure variety en route. And while all this should have culminated in a rowdy exiting of the coaches upon their arrival, the sight of the mountains bursting forth from the clear water adorned with a touch of blue that matched the sky made them all go silent.

Elizabeth shivered, overcome by the sense of tranquility and simplistic beauty that stretched out before them. It was not cold, exactly, but there was a chill in the air that she had not expected. Before she could regret not having brought a shawl with her like the others, a heavy coat was draped over her from behind, and gently pressed around her shoulders. She could not explain how she knew who it was and whispered: "Thank you, Mr. Darcy," without even turning away from the lake.

"It is thick enough that you will be warm in no time, Miss Elizabeth, and you will be spared the possibility of it clashing with your green dress."

She credited her blush to the warmth that the coat had bestowed and not to the feelings that developed when she heard only his voice and saw only the lakes. In stories, she knew, this would be a very romantic setting, and chided her senses for presenting her situation as such.

When the party turned to follow Mrs. Gardiner's direction, she saw her uncle give Mr. Darcy a quick glance before nodding and looking away. There could be no breach of propriety here, Elizabeth was cold and Mr. Darcy had only been chivalrous. Caroline Bingley, however, had evidently found something in this to disdain and so proceeded to glare at Elizabeth until she was warm enough to offer Darcy back his coat.

"Thank you," Elizabeth said to Darcy when she returned it, well apart from the rest of the group. "It was very kind of you."

"Anything for you, Miss Elizabeth," he said. "You must only say the word and my coat is yours again." He wanted nothing more than to be with her alone here. Her green eyes sparkled in the sun, her cheeks pinked attractively in the fresh air, and her smile came easily. He was completely arrested, he found, and there was no going back. He was irretrievably in love with her.

Her pink cheeks went scarlet under the intensity of his gaze and though she did not try, she would have understood his look perfectly if she had attempted it.

"Your eyes are stunning against the lake and the sky, Mr. Darcy. If I were a painter..." she began, stopping suddenly when it did not at all sound as innocent as she had meant it to.

He smiled, cherishing her lapse in propriety. "And yours, spellbinding against your dress and these mountains. Were I a poet..."

Her cheeks flushed darker than scarlet and he would have kissed her right then had her family not turned at that very moment to see where they had lost two in their party.

"Jane," Elizabeth said sternly to her sister in the dark of their room later that evening. They were to spend two nights in the Lake District and, after what Elizabeth had seen of her sister and Bingley that day, she knew that Jane must act in order to secure her happiness, to ensure Bingley that his feelings were returned.

"Yes, Lizzy?" she asked, in the same dreamy tone that she had had all afternoon.

"It is marvelous to see someone you love in love," she began, "and even better, when it is clear that those affections are returned. If Uncle Gardiner was our guardian, your hand would already be secured."

"What do you mean, Lizzy?" In truth, Jane wished that she suspected exactly what her sister meant, but was too afraid to hope.

"I mean that I have had a difficult day deciding whether you or Mr. Bingley were more in love with the other."

"Lizzy, you cannot!"

"I do, dearest Jane! And why shouldn't you? He is what every man ought to be and you, what every lady ought to be. You're a beautiful, modest, sweet, perfect, Jane."

She blushed and pressed her face against her pillow. "Do you really believe he likes me, Lizzy?"

"Who said anything about like? We were discussing love."

"You torture me. Do you really believe he loves me?" she asked from her pillow again.

"I know he loves you and I know you love him. Now —as you did not know he loves you, he does not know that his love is returned. You are too guarded, my heart. I know you are shy, but he must be made to know it, otherwise he might get hurt."

"I do not wish to see him hurt. It is only that Mama said…"

"Mama is not here," Elizabeth said curtly. "What is the harm in showing that his affections are reciprocated?"

"But, Lizzy! That is improper and…I cannot! What are you suggesting I do?"

"Follow your heart, dear sister. Do as it tells you, and all will be well."

That night, Elizabeth revisited *the kiss* in her dreams so realistically, that when she awoke, she was sure it had happened again. The words *"follow your heart,"* echoed in her head, as though her subconscious was suggesting that the dream was all part of its advice and, this idea, she did not take to very well.

She would put forth an extra effort to see Jane happy, and concentrate on that. All this talk of love was playing tricks on her memory.

"I have convinced my brother that we should accompany you!" Georgiana exclaimed, seating herself between Elizabeth and Lydia on the boat they had rented for the afternoon.

"I hope the thought has not distracted from steering," Lydia remarked, looking to the back of the boat where Darcy swung the large steering wheel.

"My brother is an excellent boatman, Lydia," Georgiana assured her.

Of course he is, Elizabeth thought, catching herself just before rolling her eyes. *Was there anything Mr. Darcy was not good at —besides first impressions?* This trip to the lakes had done nothing but highlight every perfection in him. He was knowledgeable about the land, the depth of the lakes, the wild beasts that roamed the countryside, the types of flowers that could be seen at various intervals. He had taken care to arrange their stay, their meals, and their outings and had been nothing short of *more attentive* than Mr. Bingley. While Mr. Bingley could only seem to exercise such care in the direction of one person, Mr. Darcy saw to it that all received as much attention from him, even Miss Bingley. The Gardiners, who had at first elected to separate from the "young party" as they were dubbed, decided to stay, finding their host, "too crucial a companion." Elizabeth wondered if they would be so fond of him if they had known him for as long as she had.

"Now, about Netherfield," Georgiana said excitedly, returning to the subject at hand. "I cannot get over what a coincidence it is."

Georgiana and Lydia fell into conversation while Elizabeth let her concentration and eyes roam about the lakeside, watching the water lap against the side of the boat. She could hear Jane laughing easily with Mr. Bingley, finally giving in to what was truest to her character. Bingley had certainly noticed and appreciated the change in her, allowing himself to be more caught up with her than ever. Caroline Bingley soured as soon as it was evident that Jane returned his affections but had no help from anyone in attempting to separate them. She pouted at the rear of the boat, taking turns between scowling at her brother and sizing up Mr. Darcy as he steered. The Gardiners sat beside her, cozy and happy as newlyweds.

Elizabeth let her thoughts wander to the distant memory that was Lydia's near downfall –what had been the catalyst to all of this. It was nearly a year ago that the military was stationed in Meryton, when the girls had first met Wickham and were treated to their first adolescent crush. He was handsome, charismatic, affectionate and, yet –nothing more than trash. *Can first impressions so easily give way to prejudice?* Elizabeth pondered, studying Darcy at the helm again. At first meeting, he possessed none of the qualities that recommended Wickham to any lady around him and, yet, he was now the finest gentleman of Elizabeth's acquaintance. *Yet, why is it so difficult for me to admit that?* Their eyes met in that moment and all of her unsavory thoughts vanished – replaced by nothing but an intense longing for something she could not quite place.

"Mr. Gardiner," she heard Darcy say in a gruff tone. "Would you like to try the wheel?"

Mr. Gardiner kissed his wife on the cheek and eagerly took over, saying: "I promise to avoid the shore but I cannot promise to steer away from the ducks."

"Mr. Darcy, there is room here," Caroline Bingley purred, maneuvering so that there would scarcely be a foot of space for Darcy to sit between her and the corner of the booth seat.

Without looking back, he made his way towards Elizabeth, calling back his polite decline to a disappointed Miss Bingley. "Thank you, Miss Bingley. But I believe I seat up front would suit me best."

Crushed, Miss Bingley turned her head in a huff to overlook the disappearing shore before Mrs. Gardiner drew her out of her temper tantrum by asking her about Netherfield and what decorating plans she had.

"May I?" Darcy asked, gesturing to the vacant spot by Elizabeth.

"Of course, Mr. Darcy," she answered, moving ever so slightly to her left to ensure there was enough space for him. She realized that she had miscalculated as soon as he sat down, for their thighs touched unavoidably in this position and his frame was so wide that he found it necessary to extend his arm behind her and steady himself by clasping that arm around the boat, just on the other side of her left shoulder – almost as her aunt and uncle had been seated moments before.

The same cloud of tension hung over them as pervaded the breakfast room the morning of their kiss and Elizabeth could only stand to be in such close proximity to him for a moment before letting her eyes wander down to his lips. He was letting his beard and mustache grow to fit his new, more relaxed persona of an outdoorsman and the masculine shade that the stubble cast upon his face was very attractive. Elizabeth was lost wondering what that stubble might feel like, brushing against her the way his soft face and lips had before, in the breakfast room...

He was sure of what he would say until he caught her staring at him, a captivating look of curiosity met with hunger in her eyes. Suddenly, he felt stupid having been about to ask her if she were enjoying the boat ride. He cared, of course, whether or not she did, but it was the furthest thing from either of their minds at this point. What was most relevant in his mind, of course, he could not voice –partially because there were no exact words for it and mostly because he could not kiss her here. *Not without causing a scene that would most likely anger or embarrass her*. And he could not take that risk. She deserved better. She deserved a proper courtship, a proper declaration of affections, a proper proposal…

"You are coming to Netherfield? To Meryton?" she asked, the question occurring to her as soon as she realized how much she would miss him when she went home. *I would miss him!* She realized, and then cursed herself for having fallen so hard in love before being able to reason herself out of it. *Fallen in love*, she thought. *I have fallen in love.*

"It was not my intention to run about England," he said after studying her face for a moment. "But I cannot lose the opportunity of spending every moment I can with you, Miss Elizabeth."

Her heart soared, surprised that he was saying every word and more that she wanted to hear.

"How do you think Bingley and I will be received by your mother and father?" he asked, nodding slightly to Bingley and Jane who were so wrapped up in one another that it was as if they were the only two persons in the world.

He is referring, of course, to Bingley's asking for Jane's hand, Elizabeth thought, not allowing herself to believe anything further.

"You are sure to receive a warm welcome," was all she could say, thinking of how her mother would be overbearing in such company.

"How would you introduce me?" he asked, wishing to better gauge how she would receive his attentions thus far. He was by no means (somehow) as far along with her as Bingley was with Jane, but he was a far more patient and diligent person.

"As the gentleman who has played host to three of their daughters for such an extended period of time, Mr. Darcy, your reputation proceeds you." She giggled when this answer threw him off, knowing that he had wished to hear something more complimentary but refusing to give up so easily.

"From what you said before, your father might think me a lunatic for having stood the three of you for so long –isn't that what you said?"

"It is," she said, admiring his memory, "but he would not be so unreasonable, I think. He would say that you maintained your sanity by taking his three best behaved and maybe fault you for leaving him with the other two and my mother."

Darcy laughed, enjoying this bizarre picture that Elizabeth painted of her family. "I am all too curious to meet your family, Miss Elizabeth. At times, I hope they are nothing like you say and, then again, I would be disappointed if they were not."

"You will see for yourself soon enough –that I am never wrong," she said slyly.

"Oh, I am well acquainted with that fact already, Miss Elizabeth. It is only a matter of whether I see your family in the same light."

"If not, Meryton is a small place, but there is a spectacle shop if your eyes are that bad."

She laughed and leaned her head against his arm without thinking, letting the warm sun bath her upturned face.

"My eyes work just fine," he whispered to her, taking in all of her beauty.

Chapter 27

"Mr. Darcy, your cousin is here. He will undoubtedly be bursting through these doors momentarily." Mrs. Reynolds had never been one to mince words and she was hardly ever wrong. Colonel Fitzwilliam burst through the dining room at Pemberley, surprising the entire table.

"I have impeccable timing!" he said, and, thanking Mrs. Reynolds, took a seat beside his host. He took inventory of his audience, acknowledging the Bennet girls, his niece, and the Bingleys in turn.

"You girls got sun it looks like! The lakes were beautiful, I assume?" he asked as though his entrance was anything but surprising, helping himself to the course in front of him.

"It was, Colonel, but your company was missed," Lydia explained.

"You were not stationed far from the district, I thought, Richard. So you must have enjoyed the same fortunate weather," Georgiana inserted.

"I have some news about that," he said between bites, "I was only on call for three days and spent the rest of my absence from you at my parents' estate —also not too far from the district. So you are right, dearest, loveliest cousin: the weather was heavenly." Always a jovial man —Colonel Fitzwilliam was downright ecstatic this evening.

"Where are the Gardiners?" he asked suddenly, making Caroline Bingley grimace.

"My aunt and uncle are returned home to enjoy a quiet supper to themselves," Lydia said. "They needed all their rest, they claimed, to have agreed to go anywhere else with us again."

"Go elsewhere?" he asked, looking to Darcy for an explanation and, when none came from his cousin who was too busy studying his behavior for an explanation as to his sudden arrival, looked to the others.

"I have been meaning to designate a country estate, you see," Bingley began. "And I have decided that it better suits my character," he said uncomfortably, acknowledging that it was Colonel Fitzwilliam who so often called him *flighty,* "to rent one at a time until I am fully sold on one. We, meaning the party you see before you along with the Gardiners, are to set out in the morning for an estate called Netherfield that just so happens to be on the outskirts of Meryton, where the Bennet ladies reside." There was no mistaking the look in his eyes when he looked to Jane in that moment and Richard looked between them quickly before answering.

"What a wonderful idea, Bingley. I think that suits you well. I have never been in that area myself, but if these ladies are any example as to what you can expect, I would require no further recommendation."

"I hope you will join us, Colonel," said Miss Bingley, always needing to appear the perfect hostess.

"Absolutely!" Bingley exclaimed, as though the possibility had not occurred to him before. "I know Darcy would certainly appreciate your company and I could use an extra hand in the hunt."

"You've dragged Darcy into this? Bingley, you are a miracle worker. If my cousin has agreed to go, then consider me your most obliged guest." One look at Darcy was all Colonel Fitzwilliam needed to understand *how* Bingley had convinced him to come. For it was not Bingley at all —but the object of his cousin's nearly undivided attention from across the table: Miss Elizabeth Bennet.

Colonel Fitzwilliam settled in to his usual study chair. "Well, I've been gone what —a matter of weeks? And you and Bingley have managed to all but become engaged."

When Darcy seemed to not understanding him, he rephrased, "engaged to *women* —not to each other. Bingley is not your type."

"I didn't see your wine poured at supper, how many bottles need Mrs. Reynolds order to keep up with our usual supply?"

"Sly fox!" he roared. "Bingley does not have the stomach to wait so that announcement will not take long but you —you and your iron heart, she has melted it! But the warming process takes a long time, does it not? When will you tell her? You haven't kissed her, have you?"

Darcy intended to let his cousin go on like this until he tired out but at the mention of a "kiss," he was afraid that his look had betrayed him.

"You didn't!" Richard gasped. "You?! Overcome by passion? It was the day in the breakfast room, wasn't it?!"

Darcy stood silent, aghast at his translucence.

"Should I stop bothering you?" Richard asked, wanting nothing more than to continue. "Just allow me to wish you ultimate happiness and beg you to please, *please* do not take your time. You have already, in the eyes of any onlooker. If you love her, act. You have a tendency to mull things over —this is not a financial investment, this is not a decision that requires a judge and jury. You have decided —act. Put the lady's mind and heart at rest, in the least." He stopped and looked without any sense of humor or sarcasm at his cousin who looked back at him with a sense of helpless urgency. "Do not concern yourself with worrying about whether or not your feelings are returned. She has fallen in love with you. But I still recommend that you remain on your best behavior."

Darcy's heart soared though he could not admit it. Time would tell if he would follow his cousin's advice. There was still, in his mind, much to be secured.

Darcy summoned his concentration and motioned to change the subject. "While I always appreciate your advice, I doubt that it was the sole purpose of your rather sudden appearance."

Richard was caught –knowing that he had come to say what he was about to reveal to Darcy, but not understanding how he would say it.

"Your company was not the only thing I look forward to when we steal away to Netherfield," Richard began slowly. "I have put into motion certain events that make staying in town or even at Pemberley, undesirable."

"What have you done? Your parents..." Darcy started, trying to puzzle out what Richard could have done in a matter of days with his parents. "Have you finally refused your father?"

"It is not my parents that are on the hunt for my head. In fact, there is not yet a hunt. Tomorrow, you see, will bring the hounds, for tomorrow, the paper will announce the news of my engagement."

"Your what?" Darcy demanded.

"I went to Hawkswind, Darcy, with the express purpose of seeing Anne –to see if Elizabeth had been correct about her being the same girl I remembered."

"But Richard," Darcy interrupted, fearful of what this could mean.

"You know in your heart what I've done, Darce," he said, confirming Darcy's worst fear. "And you, knowing what you do now about love...understand why I have done it. I love her, Darcy, and my love is returned. Nothing has changed between us but that we are no longer willing to deny ourselves this happiness. We discussed it at length and decided to take the...ostentatious route. I will stay out of view until our aunt's anger has calmed considerably whilst Anne will stand for the brunt of it and maintain that we must marry now that the entirety of England has been notified of it."

"And your parents?"

"I have left them a letter explaining everything and hope they understand."

Darcy sat in silence, going over the scenario in his head. He must hold to the resolve he had made to accept the decisions of those around him, but this offered him no comfort. Embracing Richard's choice did not lessen the dread he felt for what was to come. *But,* he reasoned, *even the worse outcome would be exacerbated without my support.*

"You have of me whatever I can offer, Richard," he said, crossing the study to shake his cousin's hand.

Fitzwilliam let out a quiet, nervous laugh in relief. "Then I suggest that you propose that we make haste to Netherfield."

"All aboard!" Mr. Bingley said excitedly of the three carriages that were to direct his party to his country estate. The plan was as much the same as it was on the way to the Lakes: stop as was convenient and play 'musical chairs' (as Lydia put it) to make for a diverse journey. All in all, there were ten en route to Meryton.

"From what your aunt has told me," Elizabeth's mother had said in a letter that arrived the day before their departure, *"I am to welcome a son-in-law!"*

Elizabeth hoped that her Aunt Gardiner had only waxed poetic about Mr. Bingley and Jane. *Of course,* she reasoned, *whom else could she have talked about?* It was during this lapse in concentration that Elizabeth's eyes had met with Darcy's from across the parlor and she was forced to pour over the letter as though it contained a secret message. She had felt his eyes on her long after she had broken their contact and wondered what he could be thinking about their impending departure to her home.

Everyone was subject to swapping seats on the journey except for Mr. Bingley and Jane, who would have not heard the command, had anyone the heart to issue it. Elizabeth watched, nearly laughing, as Caroline doused her brother and Jane in a fiery and menacing glare, recognizing once and for all that she was staring at her replacement and that it was beyond reversal. Just as soon as she was given a house to run as mistress of, it was taken away from her by her brother's love interest. After this realization, she was at all times (though not always physically), at Darcy's side, pushing her way into conversation here and there, never giving him a moment's peace. When he had maneuvered expertly after the second span of 'musical chairs' to Elizabeth's side, he felt it necessary to feign sleep, feeling so overcome by her remarks that it would not allow him the slightest hope of speaking with Elizabeth.

In the darkness that was his waking torment, he could hear Miss Bingley go on and on to Elizabeth about how long she had known him, how he had been exactly the gentleman she had come to expect from Bingley's letters from university and better, and something about how fortunate for the masses that he deign to show any interest in those less advantageous as he. Elizabeth handled it well, he thought, but despised hearing her in such a position. *If I had spoken my mind as Richard suggested, she would feel a great deal less uncomfortable being assured of my regard.*

As much as Elizabeth would have not liked to admit it, Darcy's theory was accurate. Though Caroline's attempts at cutting her down had never thwarted her confidence or good mood before, recognizing that she had feelings for Mr. Darcy made her more susceptible to being wounded. She now hung in a sort of limbo: owning to her feelings just hoping they'd be returned. The last thing she needed were Caroline's insults. It was easy enough to think that her feelings were sound, justified, and even returned in her own mind. But once an idea is born, there is no ignoring it. And without Darcy's encouraging looks or compliments, Caroline Bingley's words threatened to destroy it.

Frozen in his state of feigned sleep, Darcy carefully moved his hand from its resting place on his thigh to unite with Elizabeth's. He felt her jump and let a slight gasp escape when he grabbed it, squeezing it to calm her.

"A bird just flew by the window and startled me!" said Elizabeth, knowing that something must be said of her alarm.

"Was it a love bird, Lizzy?" asked Lydia with a large grin plastered across her face as she was in full view of Darcy and her sister's hands clasped together.

"I'm not an avid of scholar of bird types as our sister, Mary," Elizabeth said, squeezing Darcy's hand to indicate that everything was well. "So I cannot say whether or not it was, *Lydia*." She stressed her sister's name in hopes that she would get the hint to move on to another topic, but Caroline Bingley saw to it that the conversation continued without delay.

"That is a pity, Miss Elizabeth, for I believe that familiarizing oneself with bird types is all part of a well rounded education. Your governess should have taught you."

Darcy thought that Caroline sounded remarkably like his aunt in saying so and wished he could tell her that, as she most likely would have taken it as a compliment whilst the rest of the carriage would have known otherwise.

"We never had a governess," said Elizabeth smugly, enjoying the sight of Caroline's face turning from shock to grim satisfaction.

"Why, your mother must have been extremely occupied with your education," she said, craning her neck in hopes that she could tell if Darcy could hear her or not.

"Not at all, Miss Bingley," Elizabeth said, causing Lydia to giggle again and Georgiana to follow. It was not only this conversation that was keeping the girls entertained, Elizabeth realized, as Lydia had made Georgiana aware of Darcy and Elizabeth's public display. "We learned what we wished and allowed the others to surpass where we dared not try. If you put all the Bennet sisters together, you will have a fearsome woman as those of the *ton,* I think."

Darcy could not stand to pretend he was sleeping any longer and joined the younger girls in their laughter.

"Mr. Darcy, you cannot tell me you agree with this?" Caroline demanded.

"That the women of the *ton* are fearsome? I'm afraid Miss Elizabeth is accurate in her portrayal, more so than she probably understands." Darcy smiled at Elizabeth and pressed her hand in support.

"Mr. Darcy," Caroline said in a huff, "you have agreed wholeheartedly when I have said before that a truly accomplished lady must have a thorough knowledge of music, singing, drawing, dancing, and modern languages." She spoke with haste and desperation.

"Not all accomplished women are women of the *ton* and not women of the *ton* are accomplished, I am afraid," Darcy said. "I have given the idea a great deal of thought since and would like to expand upon what I have agreed to and say that I am not likely to prefer the company of one widely believed as accomplished to that of one who was not. If you are versed in all the languages of the world, this does not make you a more flexible conversationalist. I think a healthy amount of exercise along with an improvement in one's mind by extensive reading should be added."

Even Miss Bingley could sense that the battle was lost and so sunk into a pouting reverie whilst Lydia led the others in an animated conversation about what they could expect from Meryton. And, all the while, Darcy kept his hand firmly around Elizabeth's and, when the walk to Oakham Mount was brought up, Darcy leaned over and spoke in Elizabeth's ear, whispering:

"Since you and I are sure to awake early, I hope that you would not mind my request to accompany you to Oakham Mount alone."

She turned to him, their faces nearly close enough to kiss, and said playfully, "If you can keep up with me."

"You know, Elizabeth," he said back, closing the distance between them so that only an imperceptible space existed, "I'm beginning to fear that I will never be able to."

Chapter 28

It was early, even, for Elizabeth's standards when she awoke to meet Mr. Darcy the morning after their late night arrival. But she arose nonetheless, eager to steal a few moments away with him.

Darcy sped to their proposed meeting spot for the same purpose, astonished at how much his mood had plummeted since not sharing the same roof with Elizabeth —knowing that she was so far away. He could not —would not, stand for it much longer, as his cousin had proposed and was planning, since the second they had parted, a proposal of his own. He was determined to make himself presentable to her parents first and get to know the family better before making such a request of her father and presumably wait until after Bingley and Jane became engaged as their news was far more expected.

"Good morning, Mr. Darcy," she greeted him excitedly from yards away.

"It is indeed, Miss Elizabeth. How did you enjoy your long awaited evening home?"

She wanted to answer him honestly, say that it no longer felt like home to her, but she felt guilty in saying so. She had missed her parents, certainly, but so much had changed since she had last seen them. She knew that her heart was Darcy's and that, providing he wanted her, her place was by his side.

"I have said before that your family is truly your closest friends and relatives. I have been home since I left Longbourn, Mr. Darcy, and so nearly feel a stranger returning to it. Am I so terrible in admitting it?"

There was nothing that she was not willing to entrust to him. What was the purpose, if she could not offer everything she was to him? Was not honesty the ultimate pledge –the foundation of the ultimate bond?

Darcy could have kissed her again, offered for her right then and there. It had been exactly what he needed to hear.

"Of course not, Miss Elizabeth. I know exactly what you mean. It is as you said, your family are those you best love and it is only natural that this creates a home. When you first came to us," he began, feeling it necessary to smooth over their rough beginning before paving the way for their future, "I am afraid that I did not make your stay very homelike."

Elizabeth thought back to the harsh look she had first received from him in the dress shop. It was true –at first, it seemed that he had done everything in his power to see that she did not feel at home in his. But that was in the past.

"I am sorry," he said.

"You were only trying to protect your home, I think," she said.

"What I was attempting to do may have been noble," he said, "but the way I went about it was mistaken –to say the least."

She put her arm through his and they continued on the path to Oakham Mount, needing to say nothing more about the past. This apology clearly paved the way for a relationship unobstructed of any past misconceptions and they walked into the rising sun, acknowledging not only that it was a new day, but a new beginning.

"How I have missed you both so dearly!" Mrs. Bennet exclaimed when the Gardiners joined them for tea later. "But why have you not brought your valiant hosts?"

Darcy had already intimated to Elizabeth on their walk earlier that morning that only the Gardiners would be visiting Longbourn that afternoon. Mrs. Bennet was, of course, aware of this, but did not wish it to be so. She was not ready to entertain, but she wanted to entertain. She had threatened to die of curiosity if her daughter's suitor remain a mystery to her one moment more, especially since Lydia, whom she used to count on for gossip and details, had left so much out.

Though they had only been home a night, Elizabeth could already see Kitty forming to match her younger sister – confused by her sudden quiet and thoughtfulness, and finding nothing to do but match it. Their mother, on the other hand, seemed to grow worse without her usual, frazzled accompaniment. Without her younger sisters to school, Mary kept quiet, waiting to decide what she would next adapt to.

The Gardiners were ushered in and given refreshments despite their remaining unaccompanied and were quickly pressed for details about their gentlemen hosts. When Mrs. Bennet had heard all that could be said of Mr. Bingley, she asked of Mr. Darcy:

"What must I know about the other gentleman? I suppose I should not think he is eligible to one of my daughters as he has spent so long in their company and nothing has come of it." She allowed no one to answer before continuing, but in doing so, she missed the silent exchange between Elizabeth and her aunt. "It is a small matter, I will own. There is no harm in befriending a gentleman who can introduce you to other gentleman. After all, he was the one who introduced Jane to Mr. Bingley!"

"I nearly forgot that we bring an invitation of our own as a response to your supper invitation. The Bingleys would like to have the girls to tea tomorrow, Jane, Elizabeth, Lydia, of course, and Mary and Kitty if they are willing."

Kitty nearly bounced out of her chair in excitement, exclaiming that she would, of course, be hard pressed to deny it, but Mrs. Bennet said nothing for a long while.

"I think," she said finally, "I will need my two youngest girls tomorrow and can only spare my eldest. Jane, Elizabeth – will you consent to having tea at Netherfield tomorrow?"

"Mama!" Lydia gasped, the most she had ever fallen back into her old habits, but saying nothing more.

"Mary, Kitty, Lydia," Mrs. Bennet explained, "I will need your help preparing for our guests' arrival. I will have nothing wanting in our presentation. I am sorry you will miss your friends, Lydia, but you will be reunited with them soon enough."

Everyone was shocked at Mrs. Bennet's reasoning. It was, of course, her true plan to have Jane as alone as possible with Mr. Bingley but she had never before gone about any of her plans with such direct sense. Elizabeth felt for Lydia and would have argued with her mother, but not after seeing the look on Kitty's face. It would indeed be most unfair if only Lydia were to accompany them.

"Did you happen upon Mr. Darcy this morning?" Mrs. Gardiner asked of Elizabeth while she walked her aunt and uncle out to their carriage to return to Netherfield. When Elizabeth did not answer immediately, she added: "It is only that I recognize the same look in your eyes that I saw in his this morning...after his *lengthy walk*."

"I did," Elizabeth finally said, not knowing what her aunt would make of this confession.

"Good, I was beginning to worry too much about how much you two would miss each other." At Elizabeth's startled expression, she laughed. "Love and illness rather have the same symptoms, Lizzy, and you both look as though you should be abed. Perhaps it's better being separated, it may urge him on."

"Now you sound like my mother," Elizabeth said, laughing.

"I am allowed, at certain times. Just consider yourself fortunate that Jane and Mr. Bingley will have all her attention so that you and Mr. Darcy will have all the privacy in the world to fall in love with each other even more."

"Aunt!" Elizabeth exclaimed, turning red despite herself.

"Georgiana will be pleased at having such a sister. Actually, she will be getting many sisters. I am so proud of you, Elizabeth. I did not think it would be easy for you to find someone –and he is more marvelous than I could have hoped."

Elizabeth bid her aunt and uncle goodbye and settled in amongst her family to puzzle out her words before she was called in to her father's study.

"I have heard from your uncle and your mother, but if I want truth, I must seek you," her father said, sitting sternly across from her. "What do you think of this Mr. Bingley?"

"Surely they are to become engaged, father, and I will be all the happier afterwards. He is a wonderful gentleman, kind, considerate, and perhaps the best match for Jane. Mother will love him and, though this may not be returned with equal fervor, he will not be scared away by her as others have and may be."

"Then he has my blessing, if he can indeed get to me to request it. Knowing your mother, she will grant it upon their introduction. Mr. Gardiner says they will join us for supper tomorrow evening and then the assembly the following night. So cherish tonight, my child, as it will be the calmest from here on out. Now," he said, changing his tone from whimsical to serious, "I must definitely concern myself with your marriage prospects as I have ignored this possibility for far too long."

"You must not concern yourself with me, Papa," Elizabeth said kindly.

"I must, dear child! For there are no men good enough to have you and, yet –you must have a man, mustn't you? You have much more depth than Jane, more wit than Mary, more sense than Kitty, and more structure than Lydia, and more smarts than a man. What shall be done with you?"

"We shall have to wait for the man that does not run from me and instead fully grasps why others do not see."

It was time for Elizabeth to think of Mr. Darcy and time for her father to think of how narrowly his favorite daughter escaped the offer of Mr. Collins. His wife had been about to call them back just as his engagement to the Lucas girl was announced. Of course, Mr. Bennet wanted to see his daughter married for her safety, but he did not want to see her married on any account other than her happiness. He could not imagine a good enough man for her or even entertain the possibility that he existed.

"Marriage," he began, drawing the wisdom from his own, "is somewhat of a risk, and falling in love somewhat a myth. You fall —yes, but when you get back up, that's when the trouble begins." His had been a marriage for love, but this had dissipated quickly enough, giving way to regret and financial difficulty. Her parents' marriage was what had first made Elizabeth so cautious not only of matrimony, but of people.

"Father, I have said before that nothing could persuade me into matrimony short of the truest affection, but that is an abridged version of what I mean by this." She then went on to explain that she would not be coaxed by anything less than what she had observed for years that her parents were lacking, without saying where she had drawn her example.

Respect, admiration, care, and courtesy were amongst those things listed. It was apparent to Elizabeth from a very young age that her father knew not what he was getting himself into when he married Mrs. Bennet; she was simple minded, preferred to think only of what was right in front of her (except for, of course, the subject of matrimony, her most forward-thinking notion), and the complete opposite of Mr. Bennet's pensive and slow nature. If there had been an understanding between them, Longbourn might be a more peaceful place but, as it were, each preferred to think of the other as either ridiculous or taxing. There could be nothing done for it, Elizabeth realized, before the nest was empty. Left to themselves, her parents might stand the chance of rekindling what each had originally seen in the other.

"It seems, my dear, that you have it all figured out. But do not be so wise as to think that it is something you can understand fully from the outside. I have no doubt that you are the most learned young woman on the subject who is out of danger, but once you are in the thick of it, it can all seem quite different." Elizabeth blushed slightly, knowing this to be all too true.

"Lizzy," he continued, "just know that my answer to any young man that walks through this door asking for you will be a resounding 'no' until you can absolutely convince me of his worth. It is not as though I do not trust you to see the value of others —it is only that I fear you do not truly understand your own value."

Chapter 29

Jane and Elizabeth arrived in good time in the Bingley's carriage that was sent to retrieve them. Netherfield was a splendid house despite its lack of décor, as Caroline Bingley went to great lengths to explain the reason behind. The decorators had just been in, and the new furnishings would arrive tomorrow or the next day.

"And then we should have a ball!" exclaimed Bingley, to Caroline's soured expression.

"Let us see what we make of the assembly, brother," she said coolly. "We may have had our fill of dancing and company after tomorrow night."

As though he did not hear anything his sister said, Mr. Bingley took Jane's arm excitedly in his and led her into the sitting room to join the others. Caroline turned to Elizabeth while she hesitated to follow, saying:

"Where is the rest of your *fleet,* Miss Elizabeth? Your sisters could not join us?"

"They send their regards and their thanks, but it is just Jane and myself at leisure to join you today." She sped past Caroline towards Georgiana, not wishing to give the lady another opportunity of speaking alone with her. There was nothing to gain by such measures, but Caroline obviously did not care.

"Lizzy!" Georgiana exclaimed, jumping up to embrace her warmly. When they separated, Elizabeth saw that Colonel Fitzwilliam and Darcy had abandoned the side of the room where Caroline had been sitting to join them.

"Good afternoon," Elizabeth said, trying not to focus on one gentleman over the other. "It seems it's been much longer since I last saw you than is the case."

"You are right," Richard said, always the fastest to speak. "Have you happened to see the paper today?" There was an underlying tone of excitement in his voice, more so than usual.

"I have not," Elizabeth said as he handed it to her, beaming and pointing to an ad in the "announcement" section. Elizabeth gasped, reading of the engagement between Colonel Richard Fitzwilliam and Anne de Bourgh. "Congratulations!" Elizabeth said, embracing him before she thought better of it.

"Thank you, dear," Richard replied, happy at the genuine affection and good wishes. "It has only just come to pass. You see, when I joined you after you returned from the lakes, Anne and I had just come to an agreement. I went to see her at my parents estate –I had to know if what you said was true, and, of course, she is the same girl I knew in my youth."

"And what of your aunt? Lady Catherine?" Elizabeth asked.

"You'll understand why I was so eager to head to Netherfield. This same announcement printed in the papers will be how she learns of her own daughter's betrothal. I am in hiding until the brunt of the storm blows over. Of course, Netherfield shields Darcy as well. I can imagine Aunt Catherine on your doorstep at this very moment," Richard said laughingly to his cousin, who looked rather less bemused.

"The household is under strict orders not to let anyone inside and to accept written correspondence only," Darcy explained, "I am on a sojourn with my sister as far as the world knows." He smiled widely at Elizabeth, proud of his association with his cousin. A year ago, he may not have aided Colonel Fitzwilliam and would have most likely attempted to talk him into disassociating himself from their cousin –but he had since changed greatly.

"Marriage will be a breeze once I survive this engagement mess, eh?" Colonel Fitzwilliam joked.

"I am very happy for you, Colonel," Elizabeth said. "You must tell Miss de Bourgh that I send my congratulations and well wishes to her as well."

"She will be pleased to hear it," he said. "Georgie," he said suddenly, "what were those wild flowers you were telling me about yesterday? I should like to send some to Anne, I think, if you would be so kind as to point them out to me in the garden."

Left alone, Darcy guided Elizabeth towards the window. "How do you find Netherfield, sir?" Elizabeth asked him.

"As you have just learned, it has my gratitude as a safe haven. My aunt is unlikely to find us here. Beyond that, it is a comfortable country home."

"Nothing in comparison to Pemberley," Elizabeth said, knowing what he meant.

"I do not like to think of it as boasting of my own home, but I am only grateful that a place I love so much is mine to call my own. It is the same as my hope to call you…" he began, but got cut short by Caroline Bingley's interference.

"Miss Elizabeth, I hope you are comfortable here. I am sure it is quite a shock to be in this country after so long residing at Pemberley." It was both a jab at Elizabeth and a haphazard compliment to Darcy.

Elizabeth looked to Mr. Darcy apologetically before responding, saying: "Indeed nothing quite compares to Pemberley but, luckily, I am blessed with the same companions."

"I hope your family did not go to too much trouble preparing dinner for us this evening. We were not expecting more than a simple affair."

Elizabeth was at a loss for how to respond and so said nothing, allowing Darcy the opportunity to come to her rescue, which he had never before seen was necessary.

"Your uncle has promised us a cozy affair and a luxurious meal, Miss Elizabeth," he said. "I have heard that the market at Meryton boasts some excellent meat and cheeses."

Caroline looked as though she were about to say something but thought better of it.

"This is true so far as I have heard, but it is far beyond me to compare it to elsewhere. Our cook is very talented. If she has been able to cook for my very particular set of sisters for all our lives, distinguished guests will be nothing to her. She is determined that you leave with full and happy stomachs." She laughed at how silly this conversation was —that it could not be further from what she and Darcy had originally been discussing. Had Caroline not inserted herself in their private moment, there was no saying what would have come about.

Across the room, Jane and Mr. Bingley bent their heads closely together to discuss the possibility of Mr. Bingley hosting a ball. *Would she be pleased?* —Mr. Bingley wished to know. Jane had remained as friendly with him as she had been at Pemberley and the lakes, ignoring her mother's insights into the male mind, stressing that she must remain aloof and out of reach. Jane surmised that she would be pleased if he were to host a ball at Netherfield, providing it was not too much trouble to be arranged.

"Caroline will see to it —she has been eager to coordinate something of that magnitude," they heard him say from the window. Caroline looked, at least to Elizabeth, as though hosting a ball was the last thing she would like to do.

"At least a ball might alleviate the stress of conversing with our neighbors," Caroline observed to Mr. Darcy as though Elizabeth were not there.

"I should miss the opportunity," Darcy answered.

All throughout the visit, Miss Bingley took it upon herself to make final effort to wrestle Mr. Darcy's attention away from Elizabeth, as though she were at the advantage as his hostess. Elizabeth knew to be extra guarded around the lady for it was evident that she had one goal in mind and no limitations as to how she would obtain it. If she did not secure Darcy as her husband, she would want nothing to do with him in the future. It was all or nothing.

"So," said Richard, bouncing from the front of his feet to his heels once the gentleman were left alone, the ladies and Mr. Gardiner having gone for a short walk around the grounds, "how and when will the two of your announcements steal my thunder?"

Darcy was quicker to understand his meaning but was by no means about to answer.

"When will you propose to Miss Bennet?" he clarified for a still-stupefied Bingley.

"Oh," Bingley said, turning as red as his hair. "I wasn't going to tell either of you until after tonight, but so far, this is what I was thinking: we shall meet their parents tonight and I will make my intentions clear the morning after the assembly, having already met with them twice before. It is my intention to host a ball here in Jane's honor where we can officially announce our betrothal." Bingley smirked as though he had solved a worldwide crisis, and then added, sheepishly, "Is that all right with you, Richard? I would not wish to dwarf your news."

"Of course!" Richard boomed, laughing at Bingley's hesitation. "I thought for sure that you would beat me to the punch. That is a marvelous idea, Bingley. It does not do to wait any longer, trust me on that. Darcy —waiting is a nasty business, is it not?"

"I would have expected you to understand above any the power of impeccable timing, Colonel," Darcy said playfully, "but as you do not, I will show you by example. Timing is everything."

Bingley remained at a loss as to what was being discussed and so ran outside to meet Jane, unable to be without her for a moment longer.

"Shall we join your eager friend and the ladies, Darcy?" Richard asked. "Or is the timing not right for such an activity?"

"Richard…" Darcy began, before he was interrupted.

"Cousin, I am only giving you a hard time. I am very proud of you. You are the most stubborn bastard I have ever met; I was very disappointed when you insisted upon carrying yourself, as others would have you do. Elizabeth has opened your heart and your mind and I am eternally grateful to her for that."

"She has," was all Darcy could bring himself to say. He wanted to explain that he and Elizabeth's relationship was more complicated than that of Richard and Anne's or that of Bingley and Jane's. Richard and Anne had been a secret flame, burned for years. What Bingley and Jane shared was simple, immediate, and without difficulty. Sometimes Darcy wished that he could begin again with Elizabeth so that it would be as simple but, as this was not possible, he must dedicate himself to reversing their initial problems with care. Their kiss had only complicated matters as it had surfaced all of the simple tensions and attractions while pushing aside their unresolved discord.

He would bask in the concealment that Netherfield allowed him, protect and support his cousin, celebrate with Bingley and, finally, secure Elizabeth's hand once her father's favor and permission were obtained. He could not believe that three men living under one roof were to be engaged within a matter of weeks of one another, assuming Elizabeth would have him. He had decided to ignore the possibility that Elizabeth did not feel as strongly, for it mattered little to his cause. He would endeavor to deserve her, and if she denied him, he could not have asked for more than the opportunity to apply to her.

Chapter 30

Mrs. Bennet hid her disappointment at the announcement of Colonel Fitzwilliam's engagement as Miss Bingley hid hers concerning the introductions in general. For supper, Jane was seated between her father and Mr. Bingley in hopes that Mr. Bingley might apply for Jane's hand over appetizers. As an unavailable man, Colonel Fitzwilliam was left to attend the three youngest Bennets and Miss Bingley, while Elizabeth sat happily between Georgiana and Darcy, but unfortunately across from her mother who sat herself between the Gardiners. Fortunately, Mrs. Bennet found little else to do besides fawn over Mr. Bingley, but she would occasionally be provoked into saying something ridiculous to her other guests by Miss Bingley, whose goal it was to ridicule the Bennet family in front of Darcy.

To Elizabeth's dismay, Miss Bingley had to do very little in order to create embarrassment for them, and she could feel Darcy's discomfort from beside her. Georgiana was too kind to allow any of it to cast a shadow on an evening spent with friends and so teamed up with Colonel Fitzwilliam and the Gardiners to make it a more pleasant evening.

"It is a shame you were not here a month ago, Colonel Fitzwilliam," Mrs. Bennet said to the gentleman, wishing to illustrate how diverse Meryton was after Caroline had remarked that it couldn't be. "We had the militia stationed here for above a fortnight. I myself have never met with more entertaining gentleman. My girls were very fond of one in particular, perhaps you are familiar with him…"

"Do you know Mr. Wickham?" Kitty shouted.

"As I was saying," Mrs. Bennet continued, "Mr. Wickham was a particular favorite of ours."

With the size of the party, no one noticed the sudden draining of Georgiana, Lydia, or Elizabeth's face, nor the reddening of Fitzwilliam or Darcy's.

"He was most recently in Bath, Lydia saw him there, did you not, dear?" Mrs. Bennet demanded of her daughter.

"I did, Mama, but I have since met with much more pleasant men. Colonel Fitzwilliam, you are, by far, my favorite gentleman in a red coat."

Mrs. Bennet was confused by the affection shared between her favorite daughter and the engaged, older gentleman at her table, but said nothing of it, believing their relationship to be no more than a missed opportunity. Kitty was somewhat nonplussed at Lydia's disclosed disappointment with Wickham and so sought to talk with Colonel Fitzwilliam in hopes of gaining a fraction of the affection she had seen bestowed on her sister.

"The assembly tomorrow," Miss Bingley inserted, "should be a quiet affair then with the absence of the militia."

"Not with any Bennet lady in attendance," Mr. Bennet surmised from his seat at the head of the table, causing Darcy to chuckle. "Mr. Darcy," Mr. Bennet addressed the outburst, "I should understand if we are not joined by you. One needs a break every now and then."

Darcy laughed and answered boldly, "I would not know what to do with myself if I did. I hardly knew what to make of the silence I have experienced the past two nights at Netherfield."

"You must school me in your ways of patience," Mr. Bennet said, deciding that the gentleman needed more study than originally anticipated, especially considering the way he was prone to looking at his favorite daughter instead of at his plate.

"I have only just adopted it myself, we may learn together," Darcy said amiably.

Mr. Bennet knew not what to make of the gentleman's behavior. He was not as open as his friend, Mr. Bingley, in his affections but considering how much effort he seemed to go to in order to hide any feeling, Mr. Bennet suspected that his feelings could be just as strong. As much as he would have thought this realization would worry him, the look of disgust on the gentleman's face at his wife's behavior caused him more distress. He would not allow Elizabeth to be denied anything because of her mother's behavior.

Fortunately, Mr. Darcy was clearly very at ease with the Gardiners and so concentrated his efforts on them, and vice versa. It was not enough that Mr. Bennet now had to worry about losing his favorite daughter to a husband –it was a bigger concern that he lose his favorite daughter over a broken heart.

"Gentlemen," he addressed the bachelors, interrupting Mrs. Bennet's estimation of how it was plausible in the countryside to enjoy three dances with the same partner in one night, "while my wife will urge you to stand up with my daughters, I must speak up for the opposing side and suggest that you all twist your ankles before the first set."

Elizabeth laughed heartily at her father's joke while Mrs. Bennet made some unintelligible excuse for her husband's behavior, then added:

"Then how else might you suggest gaining a better acquaintance or otherwise making a new one?"

"I think a ball is an irrational way to gain new acquaintance," piped up Mary, seizing her opportunity. "It would be better if conversation, not dancing, were the order of the day."

Caroline Bingley seemed the biggest supporter of what Mary had said for no other purpose than to encourage her to speak more dour nonsense.

"What you propose is indeed much more rational, Miss Mary, but rather less like a ball," Caroline said once Mary was finished, affectively quieting the girl and embarrassing her family.

"I sympathize with you, Miss Mary," Fitzwilliam stepped in, "as does Mr. Darcy, I am sure. Balls seem to bring either the worst out of people, or the best out of them."

"Rather like supper tables," Darcy added to dissuade Miss Bingley from speaking again.

He disapproved wholly of what she was doing, but what perturbed him most was that he could not completely disagree with her opinion of their hosts. Mr. Bennet was kind and intelligent, but Darcy would have liked for him to show his wife more respect in front of guests; though he owned that Mrs. Bennet herself made this option nearly impossible. He had expected much more of the Bennets after having spent so much time with their daughters and the Gardiners. He often looked to his sister to make certain that she was not too uncomfortable, but he saw that she looked right at home amongst her neighbors and the bustle of the conversation. When her eyes met his, she seemed to read his worries and she gave him a warm smile, setting him more at ease.

It was with a heavy heart that Elizabeth bid their company goodbye that night, believing that, if not this, the assembly, would be the final undoing of Mr. Darcy's regard.

"That was unexpected," Fitzwilliam addressed Bingley and Darcy in the master's study later that night once Mr. Gardiner had excused himself for bed, referring to how the Bennet family had conducted themselves contrary to what was expected.

"I am still in shock," Darcy added to the observation.

"I, too, could not believe how warmly I was received! I felt no stranger to their home at all. I nearly proposed to my sweet Jane right then and there," Bingley exclaimed in ignorant bliss.

Fitzwilliam shook his head slightly when he thought that Darcy might say something.

"You will be a most welcome addition to the family, Bingley," said Fitzwilliam in his stead.

There was little talk of anything else besides the upcoming assembly, as though they may as well have joined the ladies.

"Maintain your course," was the resounding advice that Fitzwilliam left for his friends when the night was over; "do as what you thought was your best course of action before these distractions." This, he said to Bingley, but directed at Darcy.

Elizabeth approached the assembly room with equal amounts of dread and excitement. On one hand, she could never have denied herself the general splendor of such an occasion (especially surrounded by her sisters), but on the other, she could not stand seeing the look of disdain in Darcy's eyes again. It was the same she had received when they had first met, the same she had never expected to see again. She was embarrassed by her family, she always had been, but there was nothing she could do about it besides endeavor to be different –and she was.

He greeted her kindly enough, but noticed that he would stiffen when her mother was near. Rather than remain silent, as this would only cause more confusion, she decided to face the situation head on.

"I am sorry if my family makes you uncomfortable, Mr. Darcy, but there is little to be done of it, I am afraid."

This shocked him out of his reverie and he looked down. Her usual, hardened and sarcastic expression gave way slightly to a more vulnerable, hurt look. Fitzwilliam's words rang in his ears and the reassuring smile that Georgiana had given him the night previous swam before him.

"They are not as I expected," he explained sheepishly.

"They are not as you *hoped*," she accused.

"No, I..." Darcy began, before he was interrupted.

"Did it ever occur to you that they were not as I would have hoped either?" she asked, allowing her hurt to become anger. Perhaps nothing would be understood between them after all. Perhaps he had not changed. "You might be more sympathetic if you had taken into account your relatives, or perhaps you forget more easily than I the injustices wrought by Lady Catherine de Bourgh and Eric Fitzwilliam?" She took a deep breath, having said her piece, and curtseyed. "I hope you enjoy your evening, Mr. Darcy." And with that, she joined Lydia to admire the pair that Mr. Bingley and Jane made on the dance floor, while Miss Bingley assumed her place by Darcy's side.

"Miss Elizabeth is quite opinionated, is she not? I cannot decide if her company is interesting or aggravating," she said, cozying up to his side. "But I am pleased that Georgiana is so close with her, it is a pity that the Bennets do not frequent the same circles, however."

Darcy felt too much in that moment to really hear her, let alone answer. It was a difficult situation, he owned, because neither was particularly right or wrong. It was true, he should not judge so harshly as he himself was related to individuals exhibiting equally poor habits, but the source of his aversion was due to the fact that he was entertaining the idea of aligning himself with them. Neither he nor Elizabeth could help who their families were, but they *could* help what family they married into.

"It would be most improper for me to dance with anyone but you and your cousin this evening," Caroline said in hopes that Darcy would escort her to the dance floor.

"Richard does not yet have a partner, I will escort you to him," Darcy said dryly.

"William," Georgiana called once he had separated from Miss Bingley, "will you not dance at all tonight?"

"It is unlikely," he said sternly so as to not invite any more questions. His tone was not lost upon her, but she did not think it important to take this into account.

"That is unfortunate, for I see it as the best way to beginning your apology to Elizabeth as well as the only way to, at last, secure the lady's heart."

Darcy looked at his sister, so hopeful and stubborn. She could read him like a book. "Things are more complicated than you know," he said gently.

"You make things more complicated than they need to be," she persisted. "You are in love, William. Please do not break both your hearts."

The dull ache that had bothered his chest since the night before lessened slightly at the allusion to his feelings being reciprocated.

"I will dance with her, Georgie. But if I cannot amend matters, please do not lay blame with me –I will do my best."

He approached Elizabeth who stood between her father and Lydia and requested the next dance of her so that she could not deny him. As public as he wanted this exchange to be, Mr. Bennet's glare was not the type of attention he had wanted.

"Thank you, Mr. Darcy, it would be my pleasure," she said stiffly. He led her to the dance floor and they began their set, neither saying a word.

"Did you not once admit to me that you preferred conversation whilst dancing?" he asked when she did not break the silence.

"And to that, you countered that dancing would always be enough to you. Perhaps, in my silence, I was showing you courtesy."

"Then please forgive me for taking the opportunity to apologize, Miss Elizabeth. I meant no disrespect to your family and, least of all, to you."

"Thank you, Mr. Darcy," she said politely, willing herself to become less and less attached to him as they conversed. "There was no lasting harm done and I am confident we can remain friends."

This word, *friends,* was like a double-edged sword, piercing each of their chest's simultaneously. She had not wanted to say it –had waited for him to correct her, *question* her, but that moment never came. The word hung there, like the last note played of their set. Final.

Chapter 31

"Lizzy, Lizzy!" Lydia shouted from the staircase, "Mr. Bingley has come to offer for Jane!"

Elizabeth dried the reluctant tears from her eyes and reached out for her sister's eager touch, nearly matching her excitement.

"Oh, I just knew it would happen, I am so glad to have been there since the start of it," Lydia breathed.

The entire household knew of Bingley's approach by the time his knock sounded at the door so that all six awaiting Bennet ladies greeted him.

"What an excellent sight for my tired eyes this early morning. I trust you all had a pleasant slumber after last night's activities?" His voice only carried the slightest air of stress but his usual steady gaze aimed at Jane wavered, as though he were too self-conscious of it that morning. The ladies answered in turn that each enjoyed the dance immensely and that it was a pleasure to see his face again so soon afterwards so that they did not have to wonder and worry about when they would be honored by his company again.

"I trust Mr. Bennet has arisen as well?" Mr. Bingley hinted, not even having passed the threshold yet.

"He has, Mr. Bingley. You may go to him presently, and the girls and I will have tea and sandwiches ready for you when you emerge."

They dissolved into giggles as soon as his back was turned and an ecstatic Mrs. Bennet shuffled her daughters into the sitting room insisting that they should not be overheard.

The necessity of sandwiches and tea was all but forgotten and gave way to excitable curiosity at how the proposal would come about.

"Girls, we must make excuses to leave almost immediately!" Mrs. Bennet insisted after giggling with Kitty about how Mr. Bingley would struggle finding an excuse to speak to Jane alone.

"Jane," Elizabeth started, "would you like us to afford you privacy in the sitting room or would you like to ask Mr. Bingley to walk in the garden with you?"

Jane went white, suddenly overcome with the reality of the situation. "The garden, I suppose," she whispered, just as Mr. Bingley burst into the room nervously.

"Oh, Mr. Bingley!" Mrs. Bennet shouted, making him jump. "Let me call for tea!"

"Not just now," he said, fidgeting with his hat, "that is, not on my account. I am not so thirsty at the moment. But," he added, "do call for tea for you, as that was your original plan."

"Perhaps you'd enjoy a stroll in the garden," Elizabeth suggested forcefully, "Jane was just about to venture outside."

He fixed his eyes on Jane and his hands steadied. "Miss Bennet, might I accompany you?"

It was as though no one else was in the room beginning at that moment, and Mr. Bingley crossed the room to take Jane's arm and lead her outside.

"Now what?" Kitty demanded, frustrated that there could be no listening at the door when the couple was outside.

"We will watch through the window!" Mrs. Bennet announced, thrusting Mary aside to get to it first.

"Should we not award them some privacy?" Lydia suggested as Kitty joined her mother. "I doubt we shall even see them," she added hopelessly, "as the garden is rather obstructed from here once you step three yards from the house."

"Look!" Kitty shouted. "Why, they have barely cleared the doorway."

Elizabeth, Lydia, and Mary joined them at the window, overcome by curiosity. Lydia was right –if they had moved at all into the garden, the view of the couple would have been blocked. Mr. Bingley, it seemed, could not wait another moment longer and was kneeling before Jane within an arm's distance of the back door.

"How romantic!" Lydia cooed, "She looks ever so happy!"

Jane's happy tears confirmed Lydia's guess. She had obviously accepted Bingley's proposal and was in his arms in moments, embraced in a full hug. Elizabeth's eyes burned with happy tears of her own. It was the match she had always wanted for her sister, the one she deserved.

The ladies just had time to jump away from the window before the couple burst into the room and, before Bingley could even announce the news, he was overrun by the Bennet girls' well wishes and embraces.

"My son in law!" Mrs. Bennet was shouting.

"I would like to formally announce that we shall hold a ball at Netherfield in my future wife's honor," Bingley said as soon as he could get a word in.

He departed as soon as he was able, determined to make the news known at Netherfield before returning to dine with them that evening, promising to extend the invitation to others of his household as well. Elizabeth knew, somehow, that Darcy would not be in attendance. She had a curious, gnawing, dreadful feeling that last night was the last she'd ever see of him. And perhaps it was better that way, she reasoned, for she did not know how she would stand coming into contact with him again, knowing that she must not feel for him more than she did a friend. She would learn to hate the very sight of him, surely. It was best that they did not meet again.

She resolved to write to Georgiana immediately once the news of the Darcys' departure from Netherfield was made public. If she knew anything of Mr. Darcy, he would vacate the house once Bingley shared his news, unable to neither bear his friend's happiness nor stand his relation to her family. She wondered how he would handle the rage of Lady Catherine, and admittedly found this humorous. In his determination to escape her unruly relatives, he would come face to face with his very own.

There was only a short stint of celebration for Bingley's announcement before the gentleman was off again to Longbourn, dragging Caroline, and joined by the Gardiners and Georgiana. Darcy excused himself by claiming to have Pemberley business to address and Colonel Fitzwilliam stayed behind, eager to expose Darcy's real reason for staying.

When his cousin happened upon him, Darcy was half through packing his belongings.

"So this business calls you home, does it? I know it must be critical, as it risks you seeing our aunt," Richard said, challenging Darcy to tell him the truth.

"It is," Darcy said. "You won't mind staying behind with Georgie?" He had already considered taking Georgiana with him, but could not bring himself to do it. She should not suffer for his mistakes any longer. In any case, taking her away from her friends would only cause her to resent him whereas removing himself from an undesirable situation was something he hoped she'd one day understand.

"I would mind, seeing as how I deserve more than to have to explain to your sister that you are a proud, grouchy, elitist man who would rather break his own and his love's heart than to accept those he deems unworthy of his notice."

"She does not love me," he said quietly. As of last night, it had ceased to be about her family. He had just begun talking himself into becoming more accepting when Elizabeth had delivered that final blow: friendship.

"Your ignorance is working on the side of your prejudice, cousin. Elizabeth is a strong woman, she sensed that she was about to lose you and so she backed off to protect herself. You would be a fool to walk away now."

"It would be foolish to persist."

"Do you still love her?" Fitzwilliam demanded.

"Yes," Darcy breathed.

"Then do what you will, but be wary of what you might regret forever."

Colonel Fitzwilliam left on horseback to join the merry party at Longbourn, conscious of Darcy being better left alone. In truth, he also sought to give comfort where he could with both Elizabeth and Georgiana.

Chapter 32

Darcy stayed. When the happy party arrived back at Netherfield, they found Darcy's only company to have been a now-empty bottle of rum.

"If I had known that you were free enough to have finished that," Bingley said, "I would have urged you to join us."

"Then you underestimate the speed with which I enjoyed this beverage, Bingley," he said, hardly at all drunk in the context of his painful reality.

Caroline Bingley insisted upon helping him as best she could, even suggesting that she play his nurse, but the lack of inhibition the drink rewarded him aided him in fending her off.

"You will keep me company, William," Georgiana insisted, "for I am not tired at all and I insist that you drink more water before retiring. Miss Bingley, certainly we appreciate your offer, you are a most attentive hostess."

Caroline could not protest a compliment and so made her way upstairs with the others.

"You are behaving very badly, William," Georgiana said sternly. "That is all I shall have to say about your behavior as you will no doubt pay for it in the morning. Richard and I spoke about your threatening to depart and though I would like to say that I am happy to see you still with us, I am not at all pleased with *how* you are still with us."

His head swam with her admonishment, feeling bad emotionally and physically all at once.

"My best friend was in a bad mood this evening, despite her favorite sister's happy news, but I suppose this does not come as a surprise to you as it is your doing. A lover's quarrel, I understand, but you did not even have the decency to let her know how you felt before you let her down. She was confused, unsure, uncertain in her feelings, and just as she was beginning to hope they may be returned, you disappointed her and risked ever coming to any sort of understanding again. I sympathize with your disapproval of her family, but it is wrong that you should not show them respect, in the very least, for her sake. It is on the level of Miss Bingley what you have done, and I am not sorry I said that. What I am sorry for is that my best friend is confused and hurt and attempting to talk herself into hating someone she, days ago, loved with all her heart. I am sorry that my brother thinks a gentleman is a mark of social rank and not a way of conducting one's self. Go to her or leave Netherfield."

She stormed out before he said a word, leaving him to feel as though he just suffered one of the more cutting lectures from his mother. He was too drunk to attempt a ride to Longbourn and cursed himself for it.

The next thing he knew, he was knocking on Georgiana's door.

"William?" she whispered in bewilderment. "Is something wrong?"

"If I had not had so much to drink, I would be at Elizabeth's window at this very moment."

"I do not think that advisable, William."

"Exactly why I came to you. What would you have me do?"

"How many days until Mr. Bingley's ball?" she asked, yawning.

"Five," he answered. Everyone had suggested that they wait at least a month after the assembly, but Bingley would not be talked out of it happening within a week at the most. He would throw another ball, he said, the next month, and every month after that.

"I cannot give you advice when I fear that you will break her heart again, William. It is not fair."

"I will stop at nothing, Georgiana. I promise. I will do right by Elizabeth, even if she ultimately refuses me."

"Then you better begin by joining the hunt tomorrow with her father and uncle. Compliment her mother on the food that is served; observe that Meryton reminds you a bit of Lambton and that you appreciate the opportunity to explore it. Tell Mary that her dedication to the piano reminds you of your own sister. Tell Lydia and Kitty that they are the most amusing young ladies of your acquaintance. Tell Jane that she will make the loveliest bride and the best wife to Bingley. And tell Mr. Bennet that you are eager to see his library, for the praise you've heard has left you curious."

Darcy took a deep breath. "And Elizabeth?"

"Say nothing you need to go out of your way for. You must make amends with her family. She loves you, William; it was your behavior that destroyed your chances. You have five days to give Elizabeth space and earn the opportunity of speaking to her at the ball."

Chapter 33

The task that Georgiana set before Darcy did by no means come easily to him. He had become so accustomed to seeking Elizabeth's company amongst others he was surrounded by that avoiding her was like fighting a natural inclination. The Gardiners were easiest to speak to and, in time, he began to develop a sense of camaraderie with Mr. Bennet, who had at first seemed very gruff and hesitant when he was approached. He could feel Elizabeth's observant eyes on him wherever he went and amused himself with wondering whether she might be inching nearer to catch a word of what he was saying.

Miss Bingley was all at once relieved at Darcy's sudden negligence of Miss Elizabeth and utterly concerned at his attentions towards her family. All in all, the five days were the most Miss Bingley-free Darcy had ever enjoyed, as she would not dare approach him in conversation with any of the Bennets. To Jane, Miss Bingley showed some kindness, but it was in her silence that she was most polite.

"We're all fortunate that Bingley could not wait even a week to host his ball, for Miss Elizabeth is getting quite anxious," Richard observed to Darcy when it had finally come to the evening before the event.

"I'm afraid I don't take your meaning, Richard," he said as dryly as he could manage.

"I only meant to congratulate you. You're doing the right thing. I wish us both steady futures in our love lives as the past and present have been somewhat rocky."

"I could not agree with you more there," Darcy said.

"I sent Anne a post today, not able to contain myself any longer. I suppose not having heard anything from her so far is a good sign, but I cannot but help feeling uneasy."

"It is a good sign, Richard, have no fear. Anne is strong and you have given her something to fight for. Your parents' letter has been forwarded here?"

"It has –they were more shocked than anything and a bit perturbed that they were left to deal with Lady Catherine on their own, but they have extended their support."

"Good," Darcy said, patting him on the back. "Aunt Catherine will see that she has no other choice in time, it is not as though she can denounce you publicly, she is too proud to cause scandal."

"I think so too. If you were to propose to someone that the family would not under normal circumstances approve of...this next couple weeks might be best; before the storm blows over and you get all the attention."

"Perhaps we should have timed our proposals to have occurred at the same time?" Darcy asked teasingly.

"I certainly would have appreciated it," Richard said, leaving Darcy to his midnight musings of the day to come.

Chapter 34

"How lucky you are, Jane, to have a ball held in your honor!" Kitty was remarking as she wove her sister's hair into a twist of elaborate braids culminating in a large, fanning bun.

"It is nerve racking, don't forget," Jane said.

"Do not worry yourself," Lydia comforted her, "you will only be the center of attention for mere seconds only when your betrothal is announced. Before and after that, the fine décor and company will serve as a distraction."

Jane smiled, relieved at this thought, though Kitty's disappointment showed. It did not matter for what, Kitty adored being the center of attention. Lydia had shed this desire and only held that she would like to be recognized for specific and notable reasons.

"And do not forget that we will be just behind you at the announcement," Elizabeth added.

"Then I will flee to the dance floor!" Kitty announced, excited that she had already promised Charlotte Lucas' younger brother for the first set. She was not particularly fond of Charles Lucas, but it was far beyond her to discredit him for his taste.

"You and I will be swapping our partners for the second set, Kitty," Lydia reminded her, "Mr. Darcy has claimed me for the first set and Charles for the second."

"I do hope Mr. Darcy is a good dancer," Kitty said. "You danced with him surely, Elizabeth?"

"He is a fine dancer," Elizabeth answered, reeling at her sisters' mention of the gentleman's partnering with her two youngest sisters for the first two sets.

"Good," Kitty said decidedly, "then he will be a good example for Mary. I told her that he would lead her when she said that she was nervous to stand up with him."

"Mary?" Elizabeth asked, as though she had heard incorrectly.

"Yes. Mr. Darcy is to dance with Lydia, then me, then Mary. I am sure he will seek you for the set before dinner as you were not around when he was securing us."

"Perhaps," Elizabeth said thoughtfully. She could not form a coherent thought to describe how she was feeling. She could not be considered completely jealous of her sisters –that would have been ridiculous, but she did feel something akin to it. She had watched Mr. Darcy for the past four days become everything she had ever wanted and more to her family and, yet, this was all done while avoiding her. At first, she had been surprised to see him still at the mercy of Bingley and the other inhabitants of Netherfield but all this soon gave way to confusion.

He had complimented her mother on her dinner presentation, cordially accepted an invitation to see the books in her father's study, laughed effortlessly whilst seated between Lydia and Kitty, and made Mary blush with his praise. He was everything that Elizabeth had expected of him according to his recent treatment of her, yet nothing like what she had anticipated after seeing his shock at her family.

As confused as she was, she could not help but feel an overwhelming sense of excitement for this evening if for no other reason than wishing to see how events would unfold.

"Mr. Darcy might be pleasanter beneath that scowl than we give him credit for," Mr. Bennet observed to Mr. Gardiner while Elizabeth hovered just behind them. Mr. Darcy had just led a furiously blushing and silent Mrs. Bennet to the dance floor, having promised Mrs. Gardiner the next set. Mr. Gardiner looked pointedly behind them at his niece to see what she made of her father's comment while he continued, saying: "Perhaps even more agreeable than his joyous host, if it is fathomable."

"His behavior, I think, is often directed by his mood," Mr. Gardiner responded. "Mr. Bingley does not have the sort of depth that would make him susceptible to such changes. I think Mr. Darcy often has more concerns than joy, a shame for one so young. But, I think, in present company, he is learning to leave those worries behind."

"I am glad of it, having heard such praise sung from Lydia about her host. She has changed greatly, otherwise I would not have given her opinion a second thought."

"She has indeed grown," Mr. Gardiner agreed.

"Lizzy," her father asked, turning abruptly to face her, "what could have caused the change in her?"

Elizabeth swallowed hard, taking her eyes off of Darcy and her mother for the first time. "Surely it was Georgiana's influence, coupled with the close companionship of Mr. Darcy and Colonel Fitzwilliam whom she was able to see as something between brothers and friends as opposed romantic opportunities."

"I am sure you are not giving enough credit to yourself," her father said.

When the time had come for the dance before dinner, Elizabeth found herself seeking the company of Georgiana for support. She had not expected Darcy to ask her to the floor, but her sisters had put it into her mind that she ought to and she felt anxious at both the possibility of being asked and of being ignored.

She and Georgiana fell into conversation concerning the other guests in attendance when, out of the corner of her eye, Elizabeth spotted Mr. Darcy leading Caroline Bingley out to the dance floor. Her face fell and the look of disappointment was all that Georgiana required to guess at what she was feeling.

"I don't much like the idea of dancing right before dinner or even directly afterwards," Georgiana said. "Before, I am too anxious to eat and, afterwards, I am too full to dance. My brother always told me that a truly earnest gentleman will secure the last dance of the night with me and not concern himself with the superficiality of the pre-meal dance, for a meal will act as a distraction to anyone. No one wishes to be thought second to a large helping of potatoes. To seek the last dance with a lady means that a gentleman hopes that his partner will think of him just before falling asleep and will awake to that same thought first thing in the morning."

Elizabeth felt more comforted by this than she could say and, in her silence, Georgiana added:

"That is precisely why my brother said that he would escort me home early from every ball, so as to avoid this possibility entirely." Their laughter carried to the subject of their enjoyment and Miss Bingley did not at all appreciate her partner's gazing in the direction of his sister or Miss Elizabeth.

After dinner, Elizabeth set her sights on dancing every set, determined to distract herself from the unwilling object of her attention. When the evening had begun winding down and she had nearly succeeded in throwing herself into the merriment of the evening, Mr. Darcy approached her solemnly and offered her a glass of punch. To accept would mean sitting out for the second to last set but she had no concrete reason for denying him. She took it and thanked him, taking a long sip while she gathered her thoughts, attempting to compartmentalize her feelings of betrayal, jealousy, attraction, joy, and confusion so as to not let her tone become subject to them all at once. Though, separately, she owned, might be just as destructive or more so.

"If you are not otherwise engaged, I would be honored if you granted me the last dance of the night, Miss Elizabeth."

Far too much punch had found its way to her mouth and so she could not answer for an extended period of time, though it was still not enough time for her to collect her thoughts.

"Do you not wish to escort Georgiana out before the last dance commences, Mr. Darcy?" she asked, buying time. "For your sister intimated to me your concern of such affairs."

"While that is a concern of mine, I would be far more worried that your last thoughts of the evening consisted of a gentleman other than myself. I will allow Georgiana the opportunity of her first and only last dance if I am allowed the chance of what I hope will be my first, last dance of all subsequent evenings with you."

"I will put an end to your anxiety in two ways. Firstly, I will accept you. Secondly, I will point out that your sister is engaged with your cousin for the last dance, so you needn't worry about her."

"Fitzwilliam is a life saver," Darcy said, laughing. "But I shall have to admonish Georgiana for admitting my gentlemanly secrets."

"Why should kind thoughts remain secrets, Mr. Darcy? Perhaps it was only Georgiana's disclosure that won you my company in this last set."

"Then I shall thank her. But what gift will be enough to show her my gratitude? I shall have to fill every room in Pemberley with a piano."

"Your happiness is all that she desires, Mr. Darcy. She is old enough now to know what is most important."

"It still puzzles me that that could be so."

"Of course, it is always difficult to accept that those one has known since infancy are grown."

"No," he began, "I mean, yes —but that is not quite what I meant. I am at a loss to understand how she came to recognize what is most important in life before I have."

And with that, he gently took her punch glass and, placing it on a nearby tray, escorted her to the dance floor. He had requested her favorite song, a slow and moving piece that she recognized immediately and made her wonder if he could have been responsible for it. Her heart soared at the possibility, all at once relaxing at his touch and feeling startled by it. Warmth radiated through his fingers and each time the dance brought them close, she felt as though her body was being pulled closer to his. The scent of him took her back to the morning that he had kissed her so passionately and she became lost in that memory along with the present moment.

Soon enough, she was enveloped in the atmosphere that their attraction created. She was no longer Elizabeth, he was no longer Mr. Darcy —they were "we," and they moved as one across the floor.

Chapter 35

Recollection, not sleep, was the fate of Elizabeth that night. She and Jane had stayed up an hour after arriving home from the ball to discuss everything that had occurred and all that would come of her engagement.

"Oh, Lizzy! If I could see you so happy!" Jane had said, too blinded by her own glee to perceive that Elizabeth was overcome by the same sensations.

"Your happiness is mine," Elizabeth assured her.

Elizabeth rose before the sun and escaped the house to see the earliest hint of yellows across the horizon. Without a thought, her feet propelled her to the garden. She had not been there a moment before she spotted a figure approaching and she set about meeting the object of her reverie halfway.

"I could not sleep," Mr. Darcy admitted, "but it did not stop me from dreaming." He took her hands in his and held them tightly to his chest. "It occurs to me," he said, his voice shaking, "that we have not exchanged the words that we would use to describe each other as once promised."

"We have not," Elizabeth answered.

"I have a confession to make —no one word is worthy of you. So I have tried, these past months, to string several together but these still fail me. I would like to ask you for the chance to spend a lifetime by your side, so that I may show you the depths of my feeling where words fail. Would you do me the incomprehensible honor of allowing me the title of your husband?"

Elizabeth drew in a sharp and startled breath, holding back tears and squeezing his hands tightly to determine that she was not dreaming. She nodded before she was able to speak a quiet but steady: "Yes."

"As there are no words for my happiness, allow me to share this with you," he said, releasing her hands and holding her face gently, stroking her jaw line with his thumbs before gently pressing his lips against hers.

He separated from her after a moment, staring into her eyes. "This is a waking dream," he whispered, and kissed her more deeply a second time.

Mr. Bennet cleared his throat loudly from behind them and they parted with a jump.

"I apologize, sir," Mr. Darcy said hurriedly. "I should have sought your permission first..." he began.

"To kiss my daughter in broad daylight? It would have never been granted," Mr. Bennet said, looking sternly between them.

"Father..." Elizabeth began, a creeping blush replacing the whiteness of her initial shock.

"Elizabeth, please," her father urged. "Mr. Darcy, I must warn you that by any lesser circumstances, I would never part with my favorite daughter. But I see that she is quite won over."

A broad smile spread across Elizabeth's face long before Darcy realized what was being said.

"Father!" Elizabeth shouted, embracing him.

"Come inside, please, before you cause a scandal. I had better not send you away, Mr. Darcy, for I am too eager to hear your application for my daughter's hand. As part of your making amends, Mr. Darcy, I request that you stay the remainder of the day to satisfy my wife's need for an audience."

Darcy could see the extent of Mr. Bennet's wicked humor in this demand but could not, in the present circumstances, deny him.

"I would be happy to remain, Mr. Bennet, as long as I am able to send a note to Netherfield to tell them of my plans."

"Of course, Mr. Darcy," Mr. Bennet said playfully, "and, while you're at it, you may as well involve that whole party in my scheme to avoid the antics of my household and invite them to join us at their leisure."

Mr. Bennet led them to the sitting room and excused himself, saying that he would be available to Darcy in his study whenever the gentleman was ready.

"I am sorry to have caused you that embarrassment," Darcy said when they were alone.

"It was alarming so early in the day, to be sure, but it is impossible to decide whether it was more humorous or embarrassing."

He kissed her again, lightly this time, and held her close to him.

"I will go and see your father so that it is official," he said, rising to go after kissing her and placing a blanket on her lap.

"Do not let him give you too difficult a time," she bade him.

Darcy was not gone a quarter of an hour before sleep took her and he found her outstretched on the couch, snuggled beneath the blanket and pillows when he returned later. She awoke to his soft kisses and smiled warmly when her eyes focused to reveal that she was no longer dreaming.

"Good morning, my love," he said and, picking her up slightly, sat so that she could lay her head in his lap. "We have time, still, before we will be joined by anyone. Go back to sleep, Elizabeth." She nestled into his lap as he stroked her hair and, in a matter of minutes, they were both sound asleep, so relaxed at the resolution.

When Mrs. Bennet, Jane, Mary, Kitty, and Lydia came upon them two hours later, they found the couple stretched out together and slumbering so peacefully that even Mrs.

Bennet's thought it best to let them be. The ladies exited silently in awe of the circumstances and quietly petitioned at Mr. Bennet's study door for information.

"What can I say?" Mr. Bennet said, "but that my two eldest daughters are to be envied by all of England, lost in love and with the surest potential to live happily for the rest of their days."

The End

Made in the USA
Lexington, KY
18 October 2014